Right of Conquest

Conquest

ASHE BARKER

Cover Art by https://www.fiverr.com/designrans

I love to hear from my readers. Please feel free to follow me on social media.

Or you can email me direct on
ashe.barker1@gmail.com

Better still, sign up for my newsletter to be the first to hear about new releases, competitions, giveaways and other fun stuff. The link is on my website
www.ashebarker.com

Love. Hate. Honour. Obey.

It is the year 1485. King Richard III has fallen at Bosworth, his crown seized from the mud of the battlefield by Henry Tudor. The new monarch intends to stamp his authority on all of England, crushing all remaining opposition under his royal heel. And now, he has sent his men to Whitleigh…

Frances de Whytte loathes the battle-hardened, arrogant warlord who has usurped her family home, driven her brother away and now claims to own all that she holds dear. He has stolen her birthright. The House of York is ruined. But her family need her to protect them so she will do what she must to ensure the survival of those she loves.

But she will never surrender to this ferocious Tudor warrior. She would die first.

Whitleigh Castle is mine now, by right of conquest. I am now Duke of Whitleigh, a title bestowed on me at the Battle of Bosworth by a grateful king, I own this keep and all within it, including the belligerent sister of the previous duke. I intend to be master here and will particularly enjoy bringing this impudent little wench to heel.

But love and hate make odd bedfellows, and in these turbulent times who knows what alliances might form? When love and hate, honour and duty collide, and when my loyalties are tested to the limit, even I do not know what choices I might be forced to make.

Warning: This book contains sexually explicit content which is only suitable for mature readers. If such content upsets you, please do not purchase this book.

Chapter One

October 1485
Castle Whitleigh, South Devon, England

"So, how are we faring?" Edmund de Whytte, Duke of Whitleigh and the eighth to bear that title, though his claim to it now teetered in the balance, eyed his sister narrowly. "How much longer can we hold out?"

"As long as we must," came the brusque response. Frances drew in a sharp breath and fought to moderate her snappish tone. It was hardly Edmund's fault that the House of York had fallen at Bosworth two months previously, and now all of England bent under the vile yoke of Tudor rule. Neither was it her brother's fault that the wounds he had sustained on the battlefield in support of the rightful king had been superficial at best, certainly not severe enough to prevent him fleeing back here in the wake of the Yorkist defeat, to seek sanctuary in his family home.

Not his fault, even, that he had been pursued halfway across England by none other than their old enemy Richard Parnell, the Earl of Romsey. One of Henry Tudor's most loyal, not to mention most battle-hardened generals, Richard Parnell, only the second earl to bear his family's crest, had been richly rewarded for his service on the battlefield. He now claimed the title of Duke of Whitleigh by right of conquest and royal decree, along with all that went with it.

The title had been handed down through eight unbroken generations of the De Whytte family and should, by rights, pass to at least as many more. Even now, weeks after having read the royal declaration that the de Whyttes were disinherited and stripped of their titles and ancestral home, Frances refused to accept it. That upstart Henry Tudor possessed no such authority, or at least, no authority that Lady Frances de Whytte was prepared to recognise.

Castle Whitleigh was hers. *Theirs*, she corrected herself. That whoreson of an earl could huff and puff at their gates for as long as he chose to waste his time there. He would never take her home from her. She would die before she let that happen.

Edmund rose from the chair beside the cold, fireless hearth in the solar reserved for use by the family. It had been days since the last of their firewood was burned, and short of chopping up the furniture, they would have to manage without warmth. Frances chose to ignore the fact that it was only October. The season would become much chillier before long.

She stiffened when her brother, older than she was by five years, laid his hand on her shoulder. "Frankie," he murmured. "How long? Truly?"

She knew well enough that he referred to their reserves of food. Frances was just back from inspecting the pantry with Mrs Lark, their cook. It had not been a pleasant or encouraging experience. Apart from a handful of carrots and perhaps a sack and a half of flour, their larders were empty. They had slaughtered their chickens for meat, and the previous week they had eaten the last of their goats, so as well as having no eggs, no fresh milk was to be had either. And of course, due to the army camped on their doorstep, there was not the slightest prospect of bringing in what might remain of their harvest.

Indeed, as far as she could tell, the earl had helped himself to that. Frances had watched in mounting fury as enemy troops lifted potatoes, turnips, and onions from the fields she had personally supervised the planting of and helped themselves to the fruit from her orchard. She ground her teeth at the sight of lines cast into the bountiful waters of the River Tavy, knowing that they would emerge with fat, wriggling trout and succulent chub dangling from them.

All of this, while the inhabitants of the castle made do with what scraps remained to them. Soon enough, those, too, would be gone.

He means to starve us into submission, the bastard.

But that was not the response she offered to her brother. "We have some vegetables, and grain for bread. And plenty of fresh water…" Provided the earl did not realise that their source was an underground spring which he could easily enough foul if he chose to.

7

Edmund pressed her. "Apart from you and I, there are thirty souls here. Do we have enough food for everyone?"

Frances shrugged. "We shall make do. We have no choice."

"But we do." Edmund moved around to stand right in front of her. "You know what we must do. What *I* must do."

"No!" Frances shot to her feet. "You will not give yourself up, not to him."

"Frankie, I—"

"No," she repeated. "He will have you killed. Executed as a traitor."

"We must face the truth, Frankie. We must accept what has happened."

She glared at her brother through a mist of unshed tears. "I will not accept any such thing. You are no traitor. You fought for your king, as any loyal subject would."

"Unfortunately, I fought on the losing side," Edmund reminded her. "Our family, along with the entire House of York, fell to the Lancastrians. King Richard is dead, and the Tudor sits on the throne now. The world we knew is no more, and we must face this new reality."

"New reality," she scoffed. "What are you talking about? There is but one reality, and that is that Castle Whitleigh is *ours*. Our birthright. *You* are the Duke of Whitleigh, not that robbing bastard who struts about out there as though he owns the place. I will never surrender, not to him."

"Frankie, you are as fierce as a lion with the courage to match, and I love you for that, but we have to face what we cannot avoid. We cannot…" He took a deep breath, "*I* cannot cower in here while our people starve."

"But—"

He laid a finger on her lips. "Hush. And listen. I will hand myself and Whitleigh over to the earl, and in return I will insist that you and the rest of the household be left unharmed, free to leave if you wish."

"Leave?" Frances was horrified. She could not believe what she was hearing. "This is my home. I will not leave."

"Very well, I will negotiate your safety if you choose to remain. You, and our grandmother, since she is too old to move anywhere else now, and surely cannot be considered a danger to anyone, even the Tudor."

"This is madness. We should withstand this... this..."

"Siege?" he offered, not especially helpfully. "This siege that will surely end in disaster for all of us if I do nothing to end it."

"But... they will kill you." Frances bit back a sob. For all that they had quarrelled and fought their entire lives, she adored her brother and knew he felt the same way about her. And, that sentiment lay at the root of the sacrifice he was prepared to make. He was ready to die, if that was what was needed to secure the safety of those he loved.

"I will send word to Richard Parnell," Edmund continued. "I will tell him I wish to seek terms with him."

"No..." she whispered. "Please..."

"Frankie, I have made my decision. This is my responsibility. I will need you to help me do it, help me to explain to everyone, especially our grandmother. And, after I am gone, I will need you to help keep them safe."

"She shook her head. "No, no..."

"It is the only way, Frankie. We cannot hold out much longer, and I would not see this tragedy played out to the bitter end." He kissed her forehead, then turned and strode towards the door.

"Wait. I... I have an idea. There is another way."

Edmund halted and swung around to face her again. "I do not see any other way."

"There is the tunnel." Frances tipped up her chin. "It is still there. An escape route."

"The tunnel?" He shook his head. "Aye, it still exists, though I cannot say what state it might be in."

Unlike her brother, Frances could be perfectly certain what condition the tunnel was in. The secret passage was in a lamentable state of repair, but it would have to do.

The ancient escape route had been hewn a hundred years earlier, carved from the rock upon which Castle

9

Whitleigh stood so proudly. It was built in the reign of The Lionheart. The then duke, freshly returned from the Crusades, had seen such secret escape tunnels whilst campaigning in the Levant and had been sincerely impressed. He was convinced that such a facility was required to ensure the safety of his ancestral home and set about constructing it. To the best of Frances' knowledge, the tunnel had served no loftier purpose than enabling her great-grandfather to bring his many women in and out of the castle without his wife's knowledge.

"No one has passed through it for half a century, at least," Edmund reminded her. "If you are thinking to escape that way, I doubt we could get all our people through it before Sir Richard realised something was going on and ordered his men to storm our walls."

"No, not all of us. I have said, have I not, that this is my home. I will not be driven from it like a scared rabbit. But… you could escape."

"So, I am to be the scared rabbit, then?" He flashed her a smile. "Do you think so little of me, Frankie?"

"Do not be ridiculous. I am talking about escaping a senseless death. If… if your family must face the future without you, let us at least do so knowing that you are alive. And free. Spare us the necessity to see you brutally murdered, branded a traitor, and condemned to a traitor's death."

He returned and hugged her to him. "I am sorry, Frankie. I wish it had not come to this…"

"It has not. Not yet, at least." She wriggled from his embrace. "Think about it. You could pass through the tunnel and be miles away before that bastard at our gate even realises you are gone. It will be too late by then."

"Even if the tunnel is passable, where would I go? All of England is under Tudor rule."

"You could make your way to Plymouth and find a ship. Go to France, or… or…"

"Frances, this is madness. It would never work. And, what of you, of the rest left behind. There would be retribution."

"We would deny any knowledge. The earl would

10

never be able to prove anything. For all he would know, you might have slipped away through his own ranks." She paused, considering how, exactly, this might play out. "I will wait until I know you are well away, then I will surrender the castle. The earl can search all he likes, but he will find no sign of you."

"It will not go well for you, Frankie. You cannot know how he might react when he discovers his true quarry is gone."

"He will not harm me. Why would he? I am no threat."

Edmund let out a snort of disbelief.

"I am not," Frances protested. "I am merely a woman, the daughter of a defeated enemy. The most he might do is banish me."

"That would be bad enough."

She shook her head. "No, it would be nowhere near as awful as what will surely happen to you if you fall into his hands. I can plead for my life, and for the lives of our household. He is a soldier, a man of honour. He will not murder women and elderly people in cold blood, I am sure of that." She offered up a silent prayer that her brave words might not be too far off the mark.

Her change of tune did not go unnoticed. "A moment ago, he was the bastard at our gate. Make up your mind, Frankie."

Her brother was right. In truth, there was no knowing what their fate would be once Caste Whitleigh fell to the earl. But Frances was beyond desperate, ready to risk anything.

"You must escape. Please. For me, for our grandmother."

"Frankie, I—"

She sensed her victory, seized on it. "We will tell no one. You must go. Tonight, as soon as it is dark. You will take only what you can carry through the tunnel, and enough coin to get you to Plymouth and pay for a passage to France. Send word, if you can, but only if it does not place you in danger."

"We do not even know if the tunnel remains passable," he muttered.

"It does. I… I have checked."

Edmund lifted one blond eyebrow. "You have checked? When, may I ask?"

"Two days ago." She met his amused gaze. "I thought it might come to this, and that you might insist upon throwing yourself upon your sword."

"Well, not *my* sword, exactly..."

"Please, do not make light of our predicament," she snapped. "I foresaw this crisis and... I sought an alternative. I went down into the cellars to investigate if the doorway to the tunnel could still be opened. It... it took some effort, but I managed it. There has been damage. Water, I expect. The tunnel is very wet and has probably been flooded at some stage, but it is passable with care. There is a section where a wall has collapsed, but there is a space big enough to wriggle through."

Edmund let out a low oath, shaking his head in disbelief.

Frances continued, ignoring her brother's incredulous expression. "It comes out in the forest, just beyond the moat. The opening at the other end is obscured by undergrowth so is quite invisible. Even so, once out there you would have to travel quickly, under cover of darkness, get as far from here as you can before the dawn."

Edmund glanced over at the window. "It is dusk already. If I am to go along with this mad scheme of yours, I shall need to work quickly. I will require food, spare clothing, weapons..."

"I... I left supplies at the far end of the tunnel, concealed in the undergrowth. There is food, as you mentioned, though not much, obviously, just what we could spare. You will have to forage, or hunt. There is a drop of ale, a warm cloak. And boots. I left the contents of our treasury, too, or as much as might be readily portable. I could not imagine you thanking me for candlesticks and gold plate, but a pouch of silver and gold coins will not go amiss. There are our mother's jewels, also. You should sell them, and—"

"Frankie, when did you manage all of this?"

"I have been working on the plan for two days, as I

12

told you."

"Alone?"

"Of course. I have already said no one else must know." She looked to the gathering gloom visible through the window. "It is time."

The cellars beneath Castle Whitleigh were dank and cold, the only sound that of water dripping somewhere close by. Frances crouched in the clammy chill, her chin resting on her knees. The sound of her brother's footsteps had long since died away. No sound came from the inky blackness of the tunnel now, not even the scurrying of rodents. It was time to close the door again and pile some barrels against it for good measure. They would help to conceal the secret route if the cellars were searched.

And they would be. Naturally. The earl would leave not an inch of Whitleigh untouched in his determination to seek out the fugitive duke.

Frances balanced the lamp she had brought with her on an upturned barrel and put her shoulder to the stout oak door. She closed it with a soft thud. Hopefully, by the time it was discovered, if ever, it would be again obscured by cobwebs and dust, further evidence of disuse. Meanwhile, she must do what she could to hide it.

Frances spent the next hour rolling barrels across the earthen floor and stacking them in front of the door. Only when the entrance was completely hidden did she pause to pick up her lamp, dust off her grubby clothing, and make her way back up the narrow stairs leading to the scullery.

In the absence of food to cook, or a fire upon which to hang a pot, the scullery and kitchens were deserted. Frances was able to dart through unseen and made her way up the back staircase onto the first floor of the castle where the family's apartments were to be found. Her own chamber was on this floor, as was that of her grandmother and, of course, her brother when he had been in residence here. Frances stifled a sob as the reality of their situation set in.

Edmund was gone. It was unlikely she would see him again, at least not in this life.

13

Tomorrow, or the day after at the latest, she must throw open the gates of the castle and admit the enemy. Her home would be hers no longer. She would be forced to live upon the charity of others, compelled to beg the hated Earl of Romsey for permission to even remain here. She allowed herself a grim smile. How her perspective had shifted in the few short hours since she spoke with her brother in the solar.

She paused at the door to her grandmother's room. It was late. The old lady would be sleeping, but despite this, Frances could not help placing her hand on the doorknob and turning it. The door creaked open a few inches, and she stared into the darkness beyond. She could just about discern the small form in the bed. Her grandmother's gentle snores filtered through the inky blackness. Frances hesitated for a few moments, then took a step back.

"Is that you, sweetheart?"

Frances halted in her tracks. "I am sorry. I did not mean to wake you."

"I was not asleep," the old lady lied. "Is something amiss?"

"No. Nothing. I… I just…"

"Come in, child. Sit here and talk to me a while."

In the shadowed room, her grandmother struggled to sit up in the large bed. Out of habit, Francis rushed forward to assist.

"Ah, thank you, my dear." The old lady peered about her. "I do not suppose there might be a glass of water to hand?"

"Of course." Water at least was in plentiful supply. Frances poured a small cupful and held it to her grandmother's lips. "How are you this evening, Grandmêre?"

"Ah, not too bad. Sadly, there is no cure for old age, is there?"

"You are not old. Not really."

"It is only the young who would say such a thing. But, you are a sweet child, and I am glad of your good cheer. Especially in these dark times."

"Grandmêre," Frances began.

14

Lady Margaret de Whytte, dowager duchess of Whitleigh and the widow of Frances' grandfather who had died before she was even born, patted her hand. "I know, my dear."

"What? What do you know?" They had taken such care. Surely no one could possibly suspect...

"I know that we cannot continue. The siege... our food stores are depleted, and with the winter just around the corner..."

Frances nodded. This, at least, was no secret. "I have spoken with Edmund and... we have agreed that we will surrender."

The dowager nodded her acceptance of this news. "I see. When?"

"Tomorrow, probably. Perhaps the day after."

"I will come down. You will not face them alone."

"There is no need." Lady Margaret could not manage the stairs anymore and rarely ventured much beyond her own chamber. It had been months since she had eaten with her grandchildren in the main hall.

"Nonsense. You will have my support, girl, however this might end."

Frances knew better than to argue. "Thank you, Grandmère. I will be glad to have you beside me."

"Where else would I be? He is gone, then?"

"Gone?" Frances started.

"Edmund. I assume he is gone."

"He... I...." Frances was not in the habit of lying to her grandmother and did not know quite where to start.

"I was going to suggest you check whether the old tunnel could still be used. I must assume that it proved to be so."

"How did you know?" Frances whispered.

"I know *you*, lass. And your brother. I will wager he took some convincing."

Frances nodded, though her grandmother could not see her in the dark. "He did, yes."

"He is safely gone?"

"I... I think so. I hope so. I thought, if I could wait an

15

extra day before handing over the castle, Edmund would be certain to escape. He will be miles away, perhaps even at Plymouth, before anyone starts searching for him. And they would have no idea which direction to look in as there is not much likelihood that anyone will discover the other end of the tunnel and be able to follow his tracks."

"You have done well, Frankie. I am proud of you. You face the inevitable with your usual courage. But, I suggest that you might take a bath before facing the earl. Perhaps wash your hair…"

"A bath?" Frances snorted. "I do not care what he might think of my appearance or my hair. Why would I seek to impress him?"

"Not so much impress. Whatever else the man might be, the Earl of Romsey is no fool. I was thinking that you might prefer not to alert him to the fact that you have spent the last two days crawling about in the tunnel like a mole." The dowager sniffed loudly. "I hate to have to make such an observation, my dear, but you have smelled sweeter."

Frances managed a wry laugh. "I daresay. There is no fire to heat water, though."

"A cold bath never harmed anyone, lass. I suggest you get it done now, then you can crawl into bed to get warm again."

Frances kissed her grandmother. "I shall heed your advice, Grandmêre." She shivered. "A cold bath. Ugh."

Chapter Two

Frances stood on the top step, the entrance to her ancestral home standing open behind her. At her side, Lady Margaret balanced on a stout stick, her free hand tucked in Frances' elbow. The pair wore their finest clothes, having determined by mutual but unspoken agreement that this was an occasion on which they would look their best.

Light-blonde hair, gently waving but now washed and freshly braided, fell to Frances' hips. Her gown was of soft velvet in a delicate shade of blue, trimmed at the throat and cuffs with white lace. She had slippers to match, a gift from Edmund, and her mother's gold locket hung around her neck. This was the only piece of her mother's jewellery she had kept, the rest having been handed to her brother in the heavy pouch she insisted he take.

She was aware that she presented an arresting sight. This was as she had intended, since first impressions could be of vital importance. She was determined that they would not appear defeated, cowed, or even remotely subdued if she could help it. The de Whyttes retained their pride, if not much else.

She glanced up into the noon sky. The day was unseasonably warm, and a light breeze fluttered the de Whytte pennant which Frances refused to lower. Let the wretched Earl of Romsey do that, if he must.

She had sent the earl a brief note, signed to suggest it came from her brother. The note simply said that the de Whyttes were ready to discuss terms and would open the gates at twelve noon precisely. The reply had arrived promptly, equally brief.

My compliments. I look forward to our discussion. RP

RP? His initials, Frances supposed, though she did not know the given name of the earl. His family were the Parnells, a noble enough house descended, like her own, from the Normans.

Frances lifted her hand to shade her eyes and gazed across the inner courtyard to where one of her grooms hovered close to the sundial. He raised his arm, then lowered it to signal that the noon hour had arrived.

17

"Open the gate and lower the drawbridge," Frances issued the command, then stiffened her spine when the heavy portal swung outwards and the huge bridge clanked from vertical to horizontal.

"That must be him," she murmured when the figure of a large knight clad in full armour came into view. He was mounted upon a grey charger, the huge hooves pawing at the ground as the animal strained to be permitted to advance. His features were completely hidden by the visor on his helmet

"Aye, though the lad has clearly grown somewhat since last I saw him," her grandmother replied.

"You have met him before?" This was the first Frances had heard of such an occurrence.

"Yes. Many years ago," the dowager replied. "Shall we go down to meet him?"

"You need not struggle with the steps. Wait here," Frances suggested, ready to march forward to meet the conquering army face to face.

"No, lass. I said I would be at your side, and so I shall be. If you can just let me hold on to your arm…"

Slowly, the pair descended the steps. At the same time, the column of Lancastrian troops, the Earl of Romsey at the head, moved forward. It seemed to Frances that in a matter of moments her bailey was filled with mounted soldiers, all armed to the teeth and ready to murder her where she stood.

Well, so be it. She squared her shoulders and walked slowly towards their leader, her grandmother hanging on to her arm. She would meet her end with dignity, at least.

The warm breath of the stallion brushed her cheeks by the time she halted, just four feet from the Tudor warlord. She tipped up her chin and would have met his gaze but for the heavy plate concealing his face from her view.

Perhaps in recognition of that, he lifted his right hand and removed the helmet.

Frances gasped and took a step back. She had expected… not this.

The first thought to skitter through her head was that the earl was younger than she had imagined. Much, much

18

younger. In her imagination she had conjured a man of middling years at least. How could he have achieved such a fearsome reputation on the battlefield otherwise? The man before her on the mighty charger could be no more than thirty, thirty-five summers at the most.

She had expected a scarred visage, features marred by previous injuries and the hardships of a life spent in the saddle. Instead, Frances found herself gazing up into dark-brown eyes, eyes which now regarded her with a mix of interest and irritation, and keen intelligence. This man did not survive by brawn alone, that much was clear to her at first sight.

His hair, also a deep shade of brown with flecks of auburn, hung to his steel-clad shoulders. It was thick, waved around his neck, and shone in the bright sunlight. Such hair was, Frances reflected, wasted on a man.

It did not require a full suit of armour to proclaim either the stature of the earl or his powerful frame. Eying his broad shoulders, she had no doubt that his arms comprised solid muscle beneath the chain mail. His thighs, similarly protected, controlled the stallion with practiced ease. No wonder he met with such success in battle. He looked ready to take on ten men while barely breaking sweat.

Worst of all, in Frances' opinion, he was handsome. Utterly and devastatingly handsome. In other circumstances, he might actually appeal to her, and she knew she was hard to please in this respect. Not one of the potential suiters presented by her brother had met with more than a scornful dismissal, yet this man… well, she would have considered him.

Would have, had things been different. But they were not, and the sooner she got her wayward sensitivities under control, the better.

Frances' blue gaze locked with the brown. She dipped a brief curtsey, barely sufficient to signify the most grudging respect. The earl lowered his chin in acknowledgment, then leaned forward in the saddle.

"And you are?" His voice was not over loud, but compelling, nonetheless.

"I am Lady Frances de Whytte, sister to Edmund, the Duke of Whitleigh. This is my grandmother, Lady Margaret de

Whytte, dowager duchess of Whitleigh," Frances made the introductions. "Am I to assume, sir, that you are the Earl of Romsey."

"Yes, you may assume that, my lady. It is one of my titles." He cast a glance to the left, then the right. "Where is your brother, the *previous* duke?"

Did he place an accent on the word 'previous'? Frances was not certain but decided to let that pass. For now.

"I am sorry, my lord. He is not here at present." Frances held her breath.

The earl narrowed his eyes. "I beg your pardon, my lady."

"My brother is not here, sir." Frances repeated her statement, her tone hardening.

"I did not ask you where he is not, Lady Frances. I am perfectly able to determine that for myself."

Her temper flared. "Then, I suggest that you do so, my lord. Now, if you will excuse me…" She spun on her heel, intending to return to the house, only to halt at the curt command from behind her.

"Take them."

Even before she could swivel round again, Frances was seized by both arms, a burly soldier on either side of her. Lady Margaret was subjected to the same restraint.

"Let her be. Leave my grandmother alone, you bastard. She is old, and frail…" All of Frances' anger and fear was for her elderly relative. These men might do what they would with her, she was resigned to that, but she would fight tooth and nail to keep her grandmother from harm. She had promised Edmund that she would see the household safe and look how that was already working out.

Frances wriggled and fought, but her struggles were futile. She went still when a large, gauntleted hand cupped her chin.

"Cease this, Frances," the earl instructed her. "You do yourself and your kin no good by resisting or provoking me."

"Then let my grandmother be. She… she has been unwell, and—"

20

"Lady Margaret?" The earl released his grip on Frances and directed his attention toward the older woman. "We have met previously, I believe."

"Aye, we have. My husband and I were guests of your father, to celebrate his wedding to your stepmother."

At a barely perceptible hand signal from their commander, the two soldiers holding the dowager countess released her and stepped back.

"I recall the occasion well, my lady. We spoke, you and I, in the gardens. You were very kind to a confused and unhappy little boy."

"It is never easy for children. The political aspirations of adults take no account of a child missing his mother."

Frances listened to the exchange in astonishment. Just moments ago, she had learned that her grandmother knew the earl when he was younger but had been unaware that they had ever spoken.

The earl inclined his head. "Your kindness was unexpected. I have not forgotten."

"My granddaughter is older than you were then, but her confusion and grief today is every bit as cruel as was yours then. I trust you will find kindness for her, also."

"Grandmère, I—"

Frances froze at the stern expression cast her way by the powerful knight.

"There are matters I must discuss with your granddaughter, and they would be better conducted in private. Would you excuse us, please?"

The dowager bowed her grey head. "Very well. Might I prevail on your assistance…?"

"Jarvis. Piers."

The two soldiers leapt forward at their commander's summons.

"You will escort Lady Margaret indoors and see that she is settled in comfort."

"Yes, my lord." One of the men — Jarvis? — took hold of her elbow again, but Lady Margaret pulled away.

"May I place my hand just here?" she asked, slipping her fingers into the crook of his arm.

21

The flustered warrior nodded, and his colleague took up his station on the other side of the elderly woman. Frances watched, amazed, as her grandmother was assisted across the courtyard and back up the steps. The earl, too, observed their progress in silence, only directing his dark gaze to Frances when the trio were safely indoors.

"Am I to assume, in your brother's absence, that it was you who sent me that note?"

Frances nodded. "I did."

"You say that your brother is not here."

"That is correct."

"I trust you will not object if I satisfy myself regarding that claim."

"If you mean to search my home, then do so. I cannot stop you."

"No. You cannot." The earl raised his arm to beckon another of his men, the one who had followed him through the gates and had remained mounted throughout the proceedings thus far. The soldier, as heavily armed as his captain, now slid from his horse.

He, too, removed his helmet to reveal a head of jet-black hair and features that, whilst handsome, struck Frances as austere. Still, he had a look of the earl about him, too. Frances wondered if the pair were related.

The knight bowed to his leader. "I shall organise the search, Richard."

Ah, on given name terms, then…

The earl nodded. "Do so. I want this place scoured from top to bottom. The previous duke must be here, and I will have him found. Leave not an inch unsearched."

"I shall find him, have no fear." The man turned on his heel and bellowed orders at the assembled troops. Men scurried in various directions, scattering to conduct the detailed inspection required.

The earl — Richard, she now gathered — regarded Frances thoughtfully. "If I find that you have lied to me, it will not go well for you. And I have to tell you, my lady, I can conceive of no way that your brother could have left Castle

22

Whitleigh without attracting our attention. We pursued him from the field of battle. We know he came here. I witnessed him ride through that gate six weeks ago, and my troops have been camped outside ever since. Be assured, my lady, he will not elude us for long."

Frances declined to respond. What was there to say, after all? She knew perfectly well that her brother would not be discovered on the premises. Once that fact was established, the earl would change his tactics, she realised that. She had not the slightest notion what he might do, but she would meet that situation when it arose.

"Your larders will be depleted by now, I imagine."

Frances furrowed her brow. Was he about to speak to her of housekeeping? "You know full well that they are, since you stole our harvest."

The man's lip quirked. "*My* harvest, I think you will find, since the king gifted these lands to me in recognition of my service to him."

"Castle Whitleigh and the estate surrounding it belongs to us, the de Whyttes. Henry Tudor has no right to—"

"I advise silence, my lady, lest you find yourself charged with treason like your brother."

"Edmund is no traitor," Frances spat. "He is a good and honest man, a decent lord. And loyal." Her voice shook with outrage.

The earl was unmoved by her outburst. "His loyalty is misplaced, sadly. Now, about those larders… I would be glad if you would summon your cook in order that these stores can be safely laid down."

He gestured to a half dozen or so carts now trundling over the drawbridge, all laden with the spoils of the recent harvest.

"You mean to give us back our food?" Frances had not expected this.

"I never intended to deprive the castle of winter supplies since I and my troops will be in residence here from now on. I merely prevented the vegetables from rotting in the ground by having my men gather them in. Now, with the assistance of the servants, we shall see to their storage." He

23

glanced about him and caught sight of two women cowering in the doorway to an outhouse used as a laundry. "You two, come here."

Trembling, the women crept forward. Frances recognised the pair, Enid and Molly, sisters who had worked at the castle since they were young girls.

"Let them be. You have no need to frighten my servants."

"*Your* servants?" He lifted a sardonic eyebrow. "Castle Whitleigh and all who serve here are mine now." He regarded the nervous maidservants. "Show the drivers the way to the kitchen door, then help them to unload the food. See it safely stored. And you can inform whoever is in charge of the kitchens here that I expect a meal to be offered this night, one fit to welcome the new duke and his men."

"You cannot—" Frances began, only to fall silent at his glower.

Enid and Molly scuttled off, followed by the cartloads of vegetables.

His tone when next he spoke to her was cold and uncompromising. "You do not command here, Lady Frances. And you own nothing. Remember that." He addressed his next remarks to the two soldiers who still held her. "Take her inside, see that she is secured in the hall. Keep her out of my way."

Frances tugged at the ropes which bound her to the chair. The men had marched her inside and forced her to sit at the end of the high table. By way of ensuring that she did, indeed, remain out of their commander's way, they had tied her hands behind her and fastened her securely in place. Frances could no nothing but watch as her loyal household retainers, people who had served her family for generations, rushed hither and thither in response to the orders given by these invaders. Buckets of water were dragged from the well and slopped about the hall, and men set to gathering firewood in the surrounding countryside. Soon, a merry blaze danced in the hearth, though its warmth did not reach where Frances sat.

Still, there might be hot food this night, and by the looks of those wagons, plenty of it. Surely the earl would allow them all to eat.

She hoped so, or her sacrifice would have been for nothing. She wanted to live, though she realised that may be a forlorn hope. But she was determined that their people would not suffer. She would beg this hateful conqueror if she must.

Frances was not certain how long she remained pinned to the chair, observing the comings and goings about her. As far as she was aware, there had been no violence offered to her people and no resistance by the castle staff. She was glad of it. It would be futile to fight these soldiers, and Frances had no love for senseless bloodshed.

Her stomach growled when the aroma of baking bread reached her nostrils. Mrs Lark must be hard at work in the kitchens, preparing for the night's feasting. Frances allowed herself a brief moment to anticipate the first decent meal she had enjoyed in weeks.

Her musings were interrupted by heavy footsteps. She swung around to observe the earl crossing the flagged floor, followed by the man he had charged with leading the search. Neither man wore full suits of armour any longer and, if anything, their appearance was even more intimidating. The raw strength of the battle-hardened warlords was impossible to miss. And the earl did not look pleased.

Frances swallowed hard and held her breath. The earl pulled out the chair next to hers, turned it around, and straddled it.

"He is not here," he said, his tone low.

"I told you that he was not."

"You did, aye. So, my next question is, how did he escape?"

"I cannot help you, my lord. I have no notion where my brother is."

"Maybe you do not, though I doubt it. But that was not what I asked. I will repeat my question just once more. How did your brother escape from Castle Whitleigh?"

"Perhaps your siege was not as tight as you believed." She would at least try to concoct a story. "My brother knows these lands. He might easily have—"

"You try my patience, Lady Frances, and I must warn you, it is in short supply. You will tell me what I want to know, or you will answer for the consequences."

"I… I do not care what you do to me," she lied, hoping he would not detect the tremor in her voice. "I cannot help you."

"Or you will not," he corrected softly. "Very well." He exchanged a glance with his companion then tipped his chin to indicate a maid who was stoking the fire. "Start with that one."

The second-in-command nodded and crooked a finger to beckon the girl to him.

She shook her head and started to back away, only to be seized by guards who appeared from behind her. The girl was dragged, screaming, from the hall. The second-in-command followed them out.

"What are you doing? Let her go." Distraught, Frances fought against her bonds. "You bastard, what do you mean to do with her? This has nothing to do with my servants."

"I have already explained, you do not have servants any longer, Lady Frances. You have nothing at all. Now, are you ready to answer my question?"

"I… I cannot. You—"

The earl shrugged. "I see. We shall do this the hard way, then." He snapped his fingers to summon another terrified maid. "Bring me ale," he instructed.

The girl rushed off, and he turned to face Frances again. "That one will be next," he informed her calmly. "And I will continue for as long as I must."

"You are heartless. A monster."

"I am determined, this is true. And I will have what I want from you. You have only to tell me what I want to know, and all of this stops."

Frances shook her head, tears streaming down her cheeks. "I hate you. You are a murderer."

His eyes narrowed. "And you are very free with your

26

accusations, Lady Frances. Ah, I see Stephen is back. And here is my ale…"

The maid hurried innocently towards the high table, a jug of foaming ale in her hands. Meanwhile, the second-in-command strolled back through the outer door, wiping his dagger on a rag which he discarded on the table.

Sweet Jesu. The rag was smeared with blood. So much blood…

Appalled, desperate, Frances let out a strangled sob. "Very well. I will tell you. You… you win."

Chapter Three

Richard stifled any remorse. He would do what he must. Clearly, there was a secret way in and out of this sturdy little keep, and he meant to know where it was. If the previous duke was able to come and go at will, then Richard had a problem.

He did not much care for problems.

He narrowed his eyes and regarded the sobbing woman tied to the chair. "Tears will not help you, or your people. Now that we have established the gravity of the consequences should you lie to me I will ask you once more. How did your brother leave this place unseen?"

"He... he..."

"Lady Frances, my patience is not unlimited."

"Th-there is a tunnel. A secret passage..."

"Ah." He had surmised it must be something of the sort. Perhaps, given time, he would have found it for himself. But he had not that luxury if he were to give chase and, hopefully, apprehend the fugitive duke. "Where is this tunnel?"

The lady glared at him. She was making a brave attempt to stifle her sobs, though her shock and outrage were writ plain enough across her ravaged features. It was a pity, he thought, that she should have to become so distressed, but he had no alternative. Still, harassing defenceless females was not his pastime of choice, especially females as comely as this one. Her porcelain skin and pretty cornflower-blue eyes, together with the ripples of light-blonde curls escaping from her braid, created an arresting vision of the perfect English rose.

The Yorkists might be stubborn, belligerent and warlike, but they did breed exceptional women.

Richard set that thought aside, for now. He cupped her chin again, this time with his bare hand. He forced her to meet his gaze.

"Where?" he repeated.

"A... a door, off the scullery. There are stairs, leading to the cellars. It is where the barrels of ale are kept."

"The buttery. I went down there myself," interjected Stephen, his half-brother, second in authority only to himself. His dagger was now perfectly clean and re-sheathed. "I saw no door or anything resembling a tunnel."

"It is hidden…" the woman offered. "I… I will show you."

Evidently, she had abandoned further attempts to delay or generally hinder. Richard was relieved. He had no burning wish to order another poor wench to be dragged screaming from the hall.

He nodded, then gestured to Stephen. The dagger came out again. The lady let out a squeal, only to fall silent when Stephen bent to slice through the ropes holding her on the chair. He did not, though, free her wrists.

Richard grasped her by the elbow and pulled her to her feet. He was not rough. There was no need, at least not yet, to manhandle the woman. "The scullery?" he said. "I assume that to be in the vicinity of the kitchens?"

The woman stumbled at first, but Richard's hand on her arm held her upright and steady. She looked up at him but refused to acknowledge his aid. "This way," she muttered.

The cellars were damp and smelled of disuse. It was as Stephen had described; a small, narrow passageway lined with barrels. Richard grasped one and rocked it. The container was empty.

"I see we shall need to attend to the matter of ale," he observed.

"We have been unable to brew more during the siege," Lady Frances replied, her tone defiant.

Richard did not respond. Instead, he eyed the rows of stacked kegs. "So, the door to the tunnel?"

"Here." The lady inched forward, cautious of her footing in the dim light shed by the couple of torches they had brought down here to illuminate their way. "It is behind these barrels."

Richard gestured to two of the six guards who accompanied himself, Stephen, and the woman. "Shift those," he ordered.

29

Moments later, the concealed door was exposed. Richard let out a low whistle. He was impressed. It would have been difficult to locate without help. He had to assume the tunnel to be functional since the earl had, apparently, passed through it recently.

"Is it locked?" he asked.

"No. That has never seemed necessary," Lady Frances informed him.

"Open it," he commanded.

The guards grasped the handle, turned, and tugged. The door swung open to reveal a dark passageway snaking away into what seemed to Richard to be the very bowels of the earth.

"How long is it?" he asked. "Where does it emerge?"

Lady Frances hesitated, then, "It takes about fifteen minutes to reach the other end. It… it comes out in the copse on the other side of the moat."

"How long is it since your brother scuttled down here?"

"He did not 'scuttle'. You make him sound like a coward, afraid to face you."

Richard raised one eyebrow. That was, indeed, what he thought. "Did he not make his escape, leaving you and his grandmother to face the enemy on his behalf?"

"He did not want to. I begged him, pleaded with him to go."

"I see." He rather thought her version could be true. He could well imagine it. "You may live to regret your actions, my lady. And those of your brother." He paused, then, "I asked you how long it has been since your brother made his escape."

"He left the day before yesterday."

"What? Two days?" Richard swore under his breath. He had little or no chance of apprehending the man after such a lengthy head start. Still, he had to try.

"Stephen, lock her up. I shall deal with her when I return."

"L-lock me up? Not… not in the pit. Please, not there…"

Was it his imagination or did her features grow paler? It was hard to be sure in the dim light.

"The pit?" Richard looked to Stephen for clarification since his brother had personally supervised the search of the castle and was more familiar with its 'amenities'.

"I think she means a hole close to the outer wall, accessed by a trapdoor. It is perhaps twelve feet in depth. I was not sure of its purpose, but it could be used as a dungeon or prison, I suppose."

"I see. That is useful to know, but I think on this occasion we can manage well enough by confining Lady Frances to her chamber. See to it, will you? And continue to get matters organised here whilst I am away."

"Aye, Richard." His brother took Frances by the arm. "Come with me, my lady."

Richard waited until Lady Frances had been escorted back up the narrow stairs leading to the scullery, accompanied by his brother, and followed by two of the guards. The remaining four waited for further instructions.

"Come on. We will see for ourselves where this leads." Richard stepped into the tunnel first, one of the torches held aloft. He inched forward, his men falling into single file behind him.

Their progress was slow but steady for the first couple of dozen paces. Then they met with a bend to the left. Richard swung his torch about to get his bearings, then led them forward. After about twenty more paces, the dampness oozing from the earthen walls suggested to him that they were passing under the moat. Richard shivered. For all his undoubted courage on the battlefield he did not much care for confined spaces.

How long had they been in here? She had said the trip would take fifteen minutes, had she not?

"Crikey, 'tis cold as the grave in here," observed the man right behind him.

Richard could not argue but continued on until he found his way blocked by a collapsed wall. Debris obstructed the passageway, which was already quite narrow enough. Richard crouched to investigate and discovered a narrow gap at one edge. He would never have managed to get through in armour, but with a bit of excavation and a lot of determined effort, he believed they might just manage.

"Help me to widen the gap," he ordered the men, although he could see well enough that the space would only permit one of them to dig at a time.

Richard took the first turn, then stepped back to let others have a go. One of the men constantly muttered that they would likely bring the whole bloody lot down on them, a sentiment which Richard shared. But he also knew the duke must have come this way and succeeded in getting through. Had he not, they would have discovered him by now, either in the tunnel or in the castle itself.

A fluttering movement by his hip caught Richard's attention. He peered into the gloom, expecting to come face to face with a rat. Instead, he spotted a strip of green fabric, caught on a lump of rock. He plucked it free, at first believing it could have been ripped from Edmund de Whytte's clothing when he wriggled through the narrow gap. Further inspection, though, showed the fabric to be not torn cloth at all, but a ribbon. It was hardly the sort of apparel normally favoured by a fleeing duke.

Could this belong to Lady Frances?

Richard was astonished. Could it be that she had actually come through the tunnel with her brother? Had she accompanied him to the outside, seen him safely away, then made her way back alone to face their enemy?

Richard's opinion of the duke sank lower, but his grudging admiration for the courageous female grew. Such a pity that he had not made her acquaintance in better circumstances. He stuffed the ribbon in his pocket.

"My lord, I think I can scramble through now." The smallest of his men peered up at him from the widened hole.

"Try, then," Richard instructed, holding the torch closer.

In the next moment, the man hurled himself through the gap, to disappear in a scurry of dust and scrabbling boots.

"Are you all right?" Richard dropped to his haunches

to squint through the hole.

"Aye, my lord. May I have a torch?"

Richard passed him the torch, then eyed the opening with suspicion. It still looked somewhat on the snug side to him, but with a little more effort, they would all follow. "Let's get to it," he ordered. "We have wasted enough time here."

A few minutes later, having squeezed themselves through the unforgiving gap and shuffled on through the narrow passage, the waft of fresh air on his face alerted Richard to the fact that they must be close to the exit. Sure enough, they found themselves emerging into a dense thicket of undergrowth. They stumbled from the tunnel, blinking in the sunlight.

"Do we have to go back the same way, my lord?" wondered one of the men.

Richard shook his head. They could return to the castle across the drawbridge, though he did resolve to send men down to properly clear the blockage and ensure the tunnel was safe. You never did know when such a facility might prove invaluable.

A thorough inspection of the exit site yielded more clues. They came across an empty sack with the remains of some carrots within, and the crumbs of stale bread. Richard assumed the duke had chosen to carry his supplies in another bag. They also discovered one set of footprints in the damp earth, heading east, though the area immediately outside the tunnel was heavily trampled, indicating that more than one person had been there. A much smaller footprint further convinced Richard as to the identity of the duke's companion at the start of his journey.

"Which of you is the best at tracking?" he asked. Two of the men raised their hands. "Very well. You two pursue the duke's trail as far as you can. If you are able to catch up and apprehend him, there will be ample reward for you. Failing that, you will come back and report."

"Aye, my lord." They set off walking, following the direction of the tracks.

"Bring the sack," Richard commanded. "And follow me."

Stephen was in the courtyard directing the stabling of their horses. He grinned when he caught sight of his commander trudging back through the gates, flanked by two equally grimy soldiers. Richard scowled at him.

"I shall be wanting a bath," he snarled.

"Aye, I daresay." Stephen snapped his fingers to summon the closest serving lad. "Find a bathtub and set it up in the duke's chamber. We shall be needing hot water. Plenty of it." He slanted a glance at Richard. "Well, did you find any sign of him?"

"Signs, yes. He went east. I have set men to track him. But with two days' head start, I doubt they will succeed in catching up with him. I fear Edmund de Whytte has slipped past us, thanks to his sister."

"You have reason to believe she aided his escape?"

"Oh, yes. From what she already told us, I suspect it was very much her idea. And…" He pulled the green ribbon from his pocket. "I found this inside the tunnel, and footprints I suspect will be hers at the exit."

Stephen let out a long breath. "So, she was actually there. 'Tis a pity. We could have been merciful had she merely been a bystander. But this… this is treason. She aided a traitor in his escape."

"I will need to make an example of her," Richard muttered.

"Aye, or a martyr," Stephen replied.

Richard eyed him thoughtfully and nodded. "You are right. We are tasked with making peace here, not enraging the local populace. The people of Whitleigh will not take kindly to seeing their lady hanged in her own bailey. Edmund de Whytte has escaped us, and we will do nothing to aid the king's cause by venting our wrath on the women of his family. These people are vanquished, whether they accept that fact or not. The war is over, and the bloodshed has to stop."

"What do you mean to do, brother?"

"I shall speak to Lady Frances de Whytte and decide after I have heard what she has to say. First, though, I shall take that bath." He strode towards the castle entrance but halted after a few paces. He spun around to face Stephen. "Where the fuck is the duke's chamber?"

An hour later, a much cleaner and refreshed Earl of Romsey stood at the door to Lady Frances' chamber. He had retrieved the key from Stephen and now turned it in the lock. Richard pushed the door open, only to be met by a diminutive form seeking to barrel him out of the way.

He grasped her elbows and propelled her back into the room, then followed her in, back-heeling the door shut with a heavy slam. Frances glared at him, then wriggled free of his grip. Richard permitted that, for now.

"Do you not seek news of your brother?" he asked her mildly.

Frances tipped up her chin. "Did you find him?"

"You know that we did not since you were there and saw him get clean away. How long ago? Two days?"

She nodded slowly. "Yes. The day before yesterday. But I did not see…"

"Is this yours?" Richard produced the ribbon and dangled it before her.

"I… I am not sure."

She appeared perfectly sure to him. "Oh? Shall we have a look among your things, then? Perhaps we will locate its mate." Richard strolled past her to the chest beneath the window, only to spin swiftly in time to catch her when she bolted again for the door.

Richard deposited her on the large, carved bed and this time took the precaution of locking the door and pocketing the key. "Now, where had we got to? Ah, yes, your ribbon…"

"Very well, it is mine," she conceded. "But I do not see the significance."

"Do you not?" He regarded her, assessing. "Allow me to explain. It suggests that you were present in that tunnel, with your brother. I found footprints which I believe to be yours in the soft earth at the exit. You were there, with him. You assisted a traitor in escaping justice."

"I… I was not there. And Edmund is no traitor. I have

told you that."

"I realise that we disagree on that point, though the law is clear enough. And the law is not on your side, Frances, or that of your brother. As to whether you were there or not, the evidence is also plain enough. Can you provide me with any good reason why I should not put you on trial for treason?"

She blanched. "I… I did not…"

"Tell me what happened, Frances," he pressed her. Richard was reasonably certain he knew but would hear her explain it to him. "No more lies, no more avoiding. The truth, if you please."

White-faced, and still, peculiarly defiant, Frances began her tale.

"My brother is a brave man, loyal to his family and his king…"

Richard refrained from commenting.

"He… he had decided to surrender Whitleigh to you. He was concerned that our people were starving. He believed that if he gave himself up, you would not harm the rest of us."

"A noble sentiment. Why, then, is he not in chains even as we speak, on his way to London to face King Henry's justice?"

"Because I begged him not to. He is my brother. I love him. I could not bear to think that he would be murdered, brutally killed, just because he is of the House of York. I… I convinced him to escape through the tunnel."

"You assisted him in that escape, Frances. You are a traitor also." His voice was low, soft. He had no desire to frighten her further.

"Yes, I suppose I did." She glared at him, her defiance resurfacing. "And I would do the same again. I did not know if Edmund would do as I asked or not, but just in case, I checked to make sure the tunnel was passable, and I left supplies at the far end for him to pick up."

Richard was puzzled. This did not seem to be exactly as he had surmised. "When did you check the tunnel?"

"A few days ago. I had to be sure it was a viable

option before suggesting it."

"So, you were in there alone? You did not go with Edmund?"

She shook her head. "On the night he left, I went with him as far as the cellars beneath the scullery, and I waited there until I could not hear his footsteps anymore. Then, I piled barrels by the door to hide it."

"And the supplies? When did you leave those?"

"I made three trips in all, over the two days prior to speaking with Edmund. I wanted all to be in readiness so that if he agreed — when he agreed — he could go at once. If he had waited, if he had had to prepare, he would have changed his mind, I am sure of it. He was so worried about us, so reluctant to leave us... But I made him do it. I gave him no time to change his mind."

Richard walked to the window and leaned on the sill, considering all he had just heard. Beneath him, in the courtyard, his men and the people of Castle Whitleigh hurried about their allotted tasks. A man drew water from the well. Another rolled a large barrel across the courtyard and around the side of the house in the direction of the kitchens. Two maids carried linens from what he supposed must be the laundry. All so very ordinary. How quickly life reverted to normal.

And how quickly a life could be snuffed out. He knew that better than most. He had witnessed many a senseless, unnecessary death on the field of battle and had no desire to add to the tally.

Did Lady Frances' version of events change anything? To the unsympathetic observer, perhaps not. But for Richard, he fancied that the account he had heard spoke of the desperate urge to save a beloved sibling. No doubt Lady Frances hoped to keep her family home, though she had said little enough on that matter since their very first encounter. And in any case, who could blame her for that? But Richard was fairly certain that her actions had little, probably, to do with politics and everything to do with love.

And, would he not have behaved in exactly the same way had his own brother's life been at stake?

37

Lady Margaret had spoken to him of kindness and reminded him of a time when he, too, had felt lost and alone.

He turned to face the weeping woman. His decision was made.

"Frances, look at me."

He waited until she raised her tear-stained face to meet his gaze.

"I appreciate that you are loyal to your brother, but that loyalty is misplaced." He held up a hand, palm out, when she would have protested. "Listen to me, now."

She shrank back into silence. So, he continued.

"I admire loyalty, and I admire courage. You possess both, in abundance. Your actions could be deemed to be treasonous, but I see them as misguided and foolish. I also believe you to be motivated by a genuine love for your brother rather than a desire to affect the turbulent politics of this nation. You have lost your home, your wealth and position, and your family is in tatters. Your resentment is natural, and though you must learn to curb it, I will not see you die for that."

"I do not understand. You mean, I am to be freed?"

"Not exactly. Or at least, not yet. I will accept that you are no traitor, and we will agree to differ regarding your brother. Since he has evaded capture, the point is probably moot. But you have lied to me, defied my authority, sought to frustrate my taking of this house and those within by wilfully delaying your surrender until you knew I would not be able to recapture your brother. This I will not tolerate. I will have obedience, honesty, truth. If you are to remain at Castle Whitleigh, and I assume this to be your wish since your grandmother resides here, you will submit to me in these matters. You will accept that I now hold the title which was your brother's, and that Whitleigh is rightfully mine."

"You cannot expect me to—"

"Ah, but I do. I insist upon it. I will not have dissent under my roof. You will submit to my authority, and... you will accept my punishment for your misdeeds thus far."

"Punishment? But you said—"

"*My* punishment, which I think you will find somewhat more lenient than the king's justice, if a little more direct. And immediate."

"What do you mean to do with me?" she whispered, her blue eyes wide, still glistening with tears.

He moved closer, though was careful not to actually touch her. He leaned against the bedpost and regarded her stunned expression. Best to set his intentions out clearly, from the outset. "You will remove your clothing. All of it. Then you will present yourself across the foot of this bed, your bottom raised and you will receive twenty strokes with my belt. You will accept this discipline with as little fuss as you might manage. Once the twenty strokes have been administered, I will permit you the opportunity to apologise for your failings thus far and swear your allegiance to me. Should you not wish to make such an oath, we shall continue with your spanking until you do come to appreciate the wisdom in surrender."

She had been pale enough before, but her skin took on the colour of parchment now. She gaped at him as though he might have mysteriously sprouted an additional head.

"You… you mean to beat me? Until I swear allegiance to you?"

"Not beat you. Spank. It is not the same. But yes, I shall continue until I have your submission."

"And I… I will be naked?"

"Most definitely. It is the most effective way to ensure a decent spanking and the proper degree of submission." He quirked his lip. "I would think you might consider my proposal rather more acceptable than the alternative."

"What is the alternative?"

"You can leave here. I will not prevent you from doing so. You asked me earlier if I meant to set you free. I do. If you wish to enjoy that freedom here, at Whitleigh, then it will be on my terms. If you do not wish to accept those terms, you may go elsewhere."

"Where would I go? This is my home."

"I would provide an escort to see you safe to whichever of your family's homes you choose. The House of

York is defeated but not annihilated. There are plenty of your kin still enjoying their ancestral rights, having bent the knee to England's new monarch. You would have several to select from."

She shook her head. "I cannot leave my grandmother."

"You may have my word that she will not be harmed. She will be safe to live out her days here, whether you choose to stay or not."

"She... she is all I have left."

"The choice is yours," he repeated.

"Twenty strokes? I... I have never..."

At this, he raised an eyebrow. "Then the experience will be a novel one. Be assured, Frances, you will be sore. I *do* mean to hurt you, but you will survive your spanking. I will do you no lasting harm."

"No harm? You promise?"

"You have my word."

She stared at him. Long moments passed, then she shook her head. "I do not trust you. Why would I trust a man like you? You are cruel, a monster."

He narrowed his eyes. "Ah. I assume you are thinking of the girl. The serving wench...?"

She nodded. "Sara. Yes. She... she was only eighteen summers. Her mother is a widow. Sara and her young brother are all she has. Had. And you... you just..." She buried her face in her hands. "I will never swear allegiance to a man such as you. You must do with me as you think fit."

He should have anticipated this. The events in the hall earlier had not sat well with Richard, but he had become accustomed to doing as he thought needful in time of war. He did not court violence, but it had its uses. He had become hardened to the suffering, the grief caused. It seemed he must now address the consequences of his actions and seek to repair the damage.

"I shall leave you to consider your position, Frances." He marched to the door. "I will be back later, and we will speak again."

Chapter Four

Frances awoke to find her chamber swathed in the gathering darkness of early evening. The room was cold, the fire having died whilst she slept.

How long had she been asleep? Frances was unsure but thought perhaps a couple of hours. She shoved herself up on one elbow and groaned. Her spine was stiff from having slept awkwardly, and her head ached. The trauma of recent days, no doubt.

She shuddered, remembering her last encounter with the hateful Earl of Romsey. It was most odd. He had seemed almost… kind… at one stage. She had been frightened, clutching desperately at his offer of mercy, and had very nearly forgotten what a murderous ogre he really was. She had almost been drawn in by his handsome smiles and offers of a safe haven for herself and her grandmother.

It was a cruel fantasy. No one would be safe as long as they were forced to live alongside such arbitrary acts of violence. Frances' stomach churned anew when she remembered poor Sara's screams as she was dragged from the hall.

How could he? How could anyone be so heartless?

The girl was so young, just eighteen. One year younger than Frances herself.

She rolled from the bed, steadying herself against the bedpost. Her knees felt to be made of wool. And she was thirsty, her throat dry as a bone. Frances tottered over to where a small jug of water and a mug had been left on a low table. She helped herself to a long draught, then made her way back to the bed.

A soft tap on the door brought her to a halt.

Frances was reasonably certain that the earl would have locked it as he left, but she called out "Come in," anyway. To her surprise, the door swung open, and a familiar face appeared.

A face she had never expected to see again.

"Sara!" She grabbed at the bedpost. "You… you are… alive."

The maid bobbed a curtsey. "Aye, my lady."

"But… how? I saw… there was blood. The dagger…"

"I do not know about that, my lady."

"Did they… hurt you? At all?"

The girl shook her head. "I thought they would. That man, the tall one with the black hair. I was so scared."

"I know. As was I. I thought… I really believed that they had murdered you outside in the bailey, for all to see. So what happened? Really?"

"As soon as we were out of the hall, the dark-haired one told the guards to let me go. He put his hand over my mouth to stop me from making a sound, then he told me to go home. To my mother's cottage. And stay there for the rest of the day. I was to speak to no one. He… he even gave me a silver penny for my trouble, and to make up for having frightened me. He said he was sorry."

"Sorry?" Frances could barely believe her ears. "He said that?"

"Aye, my lady. He did. I was so thankful not to be hurt that I took the coin and I ran. I only came back because one of the soldiers came to our cottage and told me I was to attend you in your chamber, that you needed to see me."

"Sweet Mother of God." Frances sank onto the bed. "It was all a ruse. A cruel ploy to make me tell him where the secret tunnel was. I honestly thought he had killed you and would do the same to all my servants until I revealed what he wanted to know. And it worked. It bloody well worked."

"I am sorry, my lady."

"Oh, 'tis not your fault, Sara. You were cruelly treated, to be frightened so. But I am glad to see you safe and well." Frances peered at the maid, still not quite able to believe she was here. "You *are* well, I trust?"

"Since I expected my throat to be slit, I suppose I cannot complain. And, I do still have the silver penny. I… can I keep that, my lady?"

"Of course. You have deserved it. I just—"

"Sara, you may leave us now. And, my thanks for coming so promptly."

Frances bristled at the bland tone. The earl strolled into her chamber as though nothing untoward had taken place. He waited until the maid had scurried past him and back along the flagged corridor before turning to smile at Frances. "I trust that little reunion will have gone some way towards allaying your concerns regarding my character."

She shook her head in disbelief. "That was a cruel trick to play. To… to manipulate me so, to exploit my fears, my concern for my people. I will never forgive you for this."

He shrugged. "We do what we must. It seemed preferable to going to work with thumbscrews or extracting your teeth with a hammer."

"You are despicable," she spat.

"I am pragmatic. My tactics accomplished what needed to be done, and no one was injured in the process."

"Do you not count anguish, grief, fear as injuries? You inflicted all in fine measure, my lord."

He winced, and Frances enjoyed a fleeting sense of satisfaction. At least some of her barbs had hit home.

"I regret that it was necessary, and I hope the mental scars will fade in time."

She glared at him. "Is that it? Is that what passes for an apology?"

"I did not intend to apologise, merely explain and express regret at the upset caused. As I seem to recall you said to me not that long ago, I would do the same again if I had to."

"If you think, by parading Sara before me, that you can make me trust you, then you are very wrong."

"Trust must be earned, I know this. There is no reason, yet, that either of us should trust the other overmuch. That will come, I hope. But I will not permit you to continue to believe that I am a heartless murderer who preys on the weak, who kills for amusement, or simply because he can. Will you concede that, at least?"

Frances was at a loss. His actions were reprehensible, his deceit towering. He had led her to believe that a most vile crime had been committed and there was worse to come if she did not surrender the information he demanded. Terrified, shocked by the barbarism she had just witnessed, Frances had

43

capitulated, convinced she had no choice, only to learn that it had been a hoax. An elaborate charade. A trick.

Fury surged. She let out a shriek and flew at him, her fists hammering against his chest, seeking to gouge out his eyes if fortune might so favour her. Regardless of the names she had called him, the accusations she had hurled, she would have done murder herself in that moment, if she could.

Of course, she could not. The earl allowed her to land several hard punches, then he caught her fists in his hands and tumbled the pair of them onto the bed. Her temper spent, Frances lay still, breathless, expecting the matters to take a decidedly ugly turn.

What had she been thinking? He was three times her size. He would kill her, or worse.

To her surprise, he rolled off her to lie alongside. "I said I would return to hear your decision, Frances. So, now that you know the truth, what do you mean to do?"

"What do *I* mean to do?"

"Aye. Do you go, as I offered? Or do you stay, on the terms I explained? The choice before you is simple, I think."

"It is not simple. I need to—"

"You will decide. Now. Or I shall make the choice for you. And since you are the only one who can choose your submission, if you force me to decide, I will be sending you to the closest residence still controlled by the House of York. I believe that to be in Somerset, though you may know better."

"Somerset? The Farehams? I will not go there. John Fareham is a lecher."

"I am sorry to learn that. Even so…"

"I… I will stay."

He regarded her with interest. "You wish to remain here? At Castle Whitleigh?"

Frances flattened her lips and nodded.

"You understand my terms?"

"I am not a fool. Of course I understand. I am to be stripped naked and whipped."

He gave a mirthless chuckle. "Close enough. Do you feel sufficiently rested to endure your punishment now or

44

would you prefer to delay?"

"Delay? Why would I delay? I want it over. Done with."

"I see. Then I shall endeavour to oblige you." The earl got to his feet and offered her his hand.

"I can shift for myself, thank you." Frances sat up.

"Are you able to remove your gown, or will you require my assistance with that?"

"Am I to assume, then, that you have experience of removing a lady's clothing?"

He grinned at her. "I daresay I could manage. So?"

"I told you, I will shift for myself."

"Then proceed, please. I shall wait here until you are quite ready." He lowered himself into one of her delicate carved chairs.

Frances was convinced the legs would buckle under his weight, but they appeared sturdy enough. He smiled at her, one auburn eyebrow raised in expectation.

"Do you mean to watch me undress?"

"I do, aye."

"You have the manners of an alley cat, sir."

"Did I not speak to you previously of submission and surrender? I would add respect and civility to my requirements, Lady Frances. I recommend that you cease the name-calling and get on with undressing, before I find it necessary to increase the number of strokes to thirty."

"Bastard," she muttered, reaching for the fastenings on her bodice.

"Forty," came the response.

Frances stifled a sob and fumbled with the bronze brooch which secured her gown at the shoulder. She managed to remove it, and the fabric fell away to reveal her white linen undergarment. She had kicked off her slippers before she had scrambled onto the bed to sleep, so she faced the earl barefoot, her shift billowing about her.

"Must I remove this? It… It is cold in here."

"Shall I send for firewood?"

She shook her head. This entire ordeal was mortifying enough, without having servants parading in and out. "Just…

be quick."

Firmly staunching any sense of modesty since such sensibilities would be of no use to her now, she dragged the remaining garment over her head and dropped it in a pool on the floor. Naked, her jaw set in defiance, she met his gaze.

She fancied the earl's chestnut-coloured eyes darkened. Was that a good sign? She could not be certain. He got to his feet and slowly, deliberately, walked around her in a circle, as though to inspect her from every angle.

"Must you ogle me so?" she snapped.

Her nipples hardened in the chill, pebbling before his eyes.

"I have never, as far as I can recall, passed up an opportunity to admire a beautiful woman. I would not wish to start such a bad habit with you, Lady Frances."

"Please," she groaned. "Can we not get this over with?"

"A decent spanking should not be rushed. I intend to make this a memorable experience for you."

Frances bit down on her lower lip and wondered, if she prayed hard enough, whether the Blessed Virgin might be so gracious as to intercede and cause the floor to open and swallow her whole. At least then she would be spared this humiliating ordeal.

Sadly for Frances, the Blessed Virgin was seemingly occupied elsewhere.

His casual familiarity and undisguised appreciation of her body was nothing short of outrageous, and to find herself standing nude in his presence rendered her achingly vulnerable. She had no doubt this was his intention. He had said as much, had he not, when he made mention of requiring her to be in a suitably contrite state of mind? But whatever the circumstances, no one could accuse Frances de Whytte of being a fool. She would do what she must to get through this, and if obedience and contrition might serve as her weapons, so be it.

The earl eyed the foot of the bed. "You may require a pillow or two, in order to lift your pretty bottom high enough

46

to receive the memorable spanking I have in mind for you. Please see to that, then arrange yourself in readiness."

Faced with no better options, Frances did as she was told. She laid two pillows, one on top of the other, at the foot of the bed, then eased herself over them so the mound of goose feathers supported her stomach. Her feet barely reached the floor, and her upper body slumped above the mattress.

"I will require you to keep your hands out of the way. If you reach back, and I catch your fingers with my belt, you will likely be injured, and I cannot permit that. If you believe you might struggle to achieve this, I can help you by tying your wrists together."

Frances' stomach clenched, but she turned her head to meet his dark gaze, her resolve firm. "I will remain still," she announced. "Just do what you have to do."

"Very well. Twenty strokes."

"Twenty? I thought…" Frances bit her lip again. When would she learn the wisdom of remaining silent?

"Despite your belligerent attitude, I consider twenty to be sufficient, given the circumstances and since this is to be your first spanking at my hands. Of course, this is always provided you do not provoke me further. You are ready?"

First spanking? Surely he does not mean to do this again…

"Lady Frances?" he prompted.

She closed her eyes and nodded.

Frances was absolutely resolved to meet whatever fate was to be hers with fortitude and courage, but the sound of the belt being unbuckled, and the heavy sword being removed from it, almost unnerved her. She gritted her teeth and clenched every muscle in cringing anticipation of what the coming few minutes would bring.

She could endure this. She surely could.

But what if she could not? What if she was to faint or otherwise disgrace herself? What if she found herself begging him to stop? Would he?

She shivered, and not from the cold, though there was a distinct chill in the air. Her taut nipples were pressed into the mattress now, her hands tucked tight under her chin as she awaited the first stroke.

The whoosh of the belt whistling through the air preceded the agonising bolt of fiery pain which slithered across her skin. Frances jerked, her feet kicking up behind her, best intentions or not.

Oh, dear Lord, help me…

The earl waited a moment, just long enough for Frances to collect her wits and plant her feet back on the floor, then he swung again. The second stroke landed just above the first and forced the air from her longs.

The pain was excruciating. Just two strokes, and she was sure her skin was in flames, sizzling under the onslaught.

The air whistled again, and pain exploded beneath the first two stripes. Her stoic resolve shattered. and Frances let out a sharp cry. The urge to reach back, to protect her vulnerable backside, was nearly overwhelming.

The sound of his booted feet on the flagged floor was almost as terrifying as the horrible whistle when the belt split the air. He shifted position, raised the belt, and swung it again.

This time, the leather fell on the backs of her thighs. She would not have believed this whipping could hurt even more than had been achieved with the first strokes, but dear Christ, she had been wrong. It did. She was sobbing now, convinced she would fall into a dead faint if she had to endure more.

Seemingly, she was made of sterner stuff than she gave herself credit for. No convenient loss of her senses descended to spare her from the torment. The earl continued to rain stroke after stroke on her scorching, throbbing buttocks. Frances lost count, could manage no more than to will herself to absorb the pain as each new blow snaked across her skin, then brace for the next.

A hoarse sound erupted from her throat. It took her a moment to realise that it was her own voice, pleading for him to stop, promising to do anything, say anything, if he would just stop.

He did, briefly, but only to speak to her.

"You are doing well, Frances. That was the fifteenth

48

stroke. Just five left. Do you need a drink? Some water?"

She shook her head, only dimly aware of his words but understanding enough to appreciate that her ordeal was not over. There was more…

"Please, just do it. I… I cannot…"

He laid his palm on her smarting buttock and rubbed slowly. "You can. You are a grown woman, not a child. You earned this spanking. You can endure it. I will not force you beyond that which you can manage."

"H-how would you know?" she ground out.

"I will know," he asserted. "You do not trust me, yet, but you will learn to. So, we continue?"

She nodded into the mattress. He laid his palm on her other buttock to repeat the same stroking motion. Frances winced. Did he think to massage the agony right into her skin, force it deep into her flesh?

Even so, she was strangely bereft when his touch deserted her. The contact had been somehow soothing, reassuring her that she had not been abandoned in this world of darkness and pain.

She cried out at the mere sound of the belt this time, even before the leather wrapped itself around her tender flesh. She was convinced she was about the heave up her breakfast, but mercifully she was spared that indignity. The belt soared again and sent another wave of agony across her scorched bottom.

How many is that? She struggled to remember what he had said mere moments ago.

"Aaagh!" She could not contain the piercing scream which surged from her throat when the next stroke fell, again across her thighs. *Please, not there. Not there…*

But the earl knew better. He chose his spot well, for maximum impact. Another stroke landed just a fraction below the last one. Her entire bottom and thighs were surely on fire now. She could almost smell the flames. Her screams blended into each other as Frances squirmed and writhed under the relentless spanking.

No more. Surely, no more…

"Oh God, please… please…" she muttered between

49

screams. "I am sorry, I am sorry. I swear it."

"I am glad to hear it. Perhaps we will not require to continue after all. Am I to understand that you are now ready to pledge your allegiance to me and to the Tudor king?"

There was a slap and the leather landed on the floor by her feet. Frances could scarcely believe it. Was it over? Had she, despite her fears, really managed to survive?

"Frances? Are you ready to take your oath?" His tone had hardened, she was sure of that. He expected an answer.

She had no answer for him. Frances was not ready, not nearly. There was... too much confusion, too much turmoil. She hurt so much that she could barely think straight, would have struggled to recall her own name, let alone that of the man who now claimed to be the monarch. For sure, she could not string a coherent oath of allegiance together.

"I... I am not certain. I just..."

"Here. Drink this."

A mug of fresh water was pressed against her parched lips. Frances had not even realised she was thirsty until the deliciously cool liquid slid down her throat. She grasped the earl's wrist and held on so he would not remove the cup.

He waited until she stopped drinking before setting the cup aside. "Frances, you will look at me now."

Would she? He certainly seemed to think so, though her eyelids had a different notion. They remained tightly shut.

"Look at me." That stern tone again, that uncompromising insistence upon obedience. She had no choice...

His features came into view when her eyelids reluctantly parted. The earl crouched before her, his face on the same level as hers. He smiled at her, and there was warmth there. Kindness, too, though she would not have believed it possible.

She reached out, stroked his chin with the tips of her fingers. It was the first time she had voluntarily touched him. "Is it over? Truly?"

"Almost, if you want it to be. You have but to swear you will obey and accept my authority here."

"And the king…?"

"Perhaps we can leave His Majesty for another day. Do *I* have your allegiance, Frances?"

"Only you? Then, yes. I… I will obey and… and…" Her eyelids closed again. "I am tired."

"I know. You may sleep now if you wish. Would you like me to send a servant to attend you?"

She shook her head. Her misery was already perfectly complete. She did not require the addition of witnesses to see her reduced to this quivering, weeping wreck.

"As you like. I shall leave you, then. You will not be disturbed."

He straightened, and was about to turn away, but she reached out and grasped his sleeve. "Please, do not go."

He paused. "Lady Frances? We are done here."

"Please, do not leave me alone." She could not explain, not to herself, and most certainly not to this man who she loathed but could not bear to be parted from. "I do not want to be alone. Not yet…"

He seemed to hesitate, then made up his mind. He reached behind her to drag a blanket from the bed and draped that around her naked shoulders. Then he lifted her in his arms and carried her to the chair he had occupied earlier, whilst he had watched her undress. He arranged her in his lap, her weight tilted to one side in order to spare her sore bottom, and he simply held her.

"Why are you being nice?" A silly question, perhaps. She should just be glad of his kindness. It was, after all, most pleasant to be cradled in this manner, protected from… everything.

"Why would I not? You have accepted your punishment and sworn allegiance to me. I have no further quarrel with you."

"I… I hate you," she murmured, her eyelids drooping of their own accord.

"Maybe you do, a little. Sleep now, Frances."

She let out a contented sigh, sniffled, and settled in against his broad chest. The last thing she remembered, she thought, though she could not be sure, was the gentle motion

51

as he carried her back to the bed, and the light touch of his hand on her hair, followed by the soft closing of the door.

Chapter Five

He raised his hand to knock, then lowered it again. This was his home. He was lord here now and required no permission to enter any part of Castle Whitleigh. Richard shrugged and tapped on the oak panel anyway.

A faint voice from within bade him enter. He opened the door and stepped inside.

"Am I disturbing you?"

The dowager countess sat in a chair by her window. She started to rise when he entered.

Richard gestured to her to remain where she was. "I had hoped to speak with you, Lady Margaret."

She settled back and nodded. "Of course. I... may I offer you some refreshment? We have not much... the siege, you will understand, but I believe there may be some ale..."

"I took the liberty of bringing wine." He deposited a jug on a small table to the lady's right, along with two earthenware goblets.

"Ah." She smiled. "A rare treat. I believe you may be the perfect guest."

Richard poured them both a measure of the claret and handed one to the elderly dowager. "I trust you have not suffered unduly as a result of this day's events."

She sipped her wine, then shook her head. "When you reach my age, a little excitement does not go amiss, though I am relieved that events transpired without bloodshed... despite first appearances. I believe I have you to thank for that."

"I confess, my life thus far has been one of violence and conflict. I do not shy away from what is needful, but neither do I make war on women and unarmed villagers."

"Young Sara may have a different tale to tell. I gather she was near faint with terror when she was dragged from the hall."

"If you have heard that tale, you will be aware that she was not harmed."

Lady Margaret fixed him with a fierce, disapproving glare. "It was a despicable deception. That poor girl..."

Was it? Perhaps, but Richard was unrepentant. "It

achieved what was required, and it avoided the need for the genuine bloodshed you so deplore. The girl was compensated, and my brother apologised for the distress caused. I suggest we consider the matter closed and move on."

"I do not believe I am quite ready to do so. If you and I are to deal well together, I must know that you are to be trusted."

"You doubt my honour, Lady Margaret?"

"I do not wish to, but your tactics earlier were callous and cruel."

Richard narrowed his eyes but did not interrupt. He was unaccustomed to being berated by those he had vanquished but he felt obliged, on this occasion, to allow the elderly woman her say.

The dowager continued, her expression stern. "You must know as well as I do that your power here is absolute. You have no need to resort to such brutality in order to make your point."

In general, Richard would agree, though he still considered his actions preferable to some of the alternatives. He had needed information, and he had needed it quickly. He had used Lady Frances' obvious care and concern for her household as a weapon against her, and it had worked. He took no pride in it, but neither did he truly regret his choices.

"May I have your assurance that such… incidents will not become commonplace here? I do not believe the nerves of our servants will stand it." Lady Margaret glowered at him.

He could accede to this, more or less. "Provided I encounter no resistance, no one need be injured, and life here may continue much as it did before."

She sipped again, then met his gaze. "Very well. But there is another matter of concern to me which I must raise with you. I heard my granddaughter's screams earlier."

Richard nodded. He supposed she would have. The entire household probably heard Frances' caterwauling, and much of the surrounding countryside, too.

"I ventured along the corridor to check on her," the old lady continued.

"I see."

"I expected the door to be locked, but it was not."

"Lady Frances is not a prisoner. She has… accepted the changed circumstances here at Castle Whitleigh, and we have arrived at an understanding."

"I could see that. She will be sore for days to come."

"Aye, I expect so." Again, he would not apologise for doing what had been needful. In truth, the girl had got off lightly. He could have handed her over to the king's forces, and her fate then would have been death in all probability. "Did you speak with her?"

Lady Margaret shook her head. "She was asleep, so I placed a blanket over her and let her be. I trust you will have no objection if I tend her bruises with a salve tomorrow?"

"I see no harm in that. Her lesson has been learned. She did well, and I would not prolong her suffering."

The dowager nodded, deep in thought. "Frances is stubborn, and proud, and so headstrong it terrifies me on occasions. I… I would ask you to be patient with her. She will accept that which she cannot change, I know it, but it will take time. I hope you do not mean to ill-treat her."

He gazed into his wine for several moments, then, "I *will* be master here, Lady Margaret, and I will do what I must to ensure this is clearly understood. I believe matters to be resolved between myself and your granddaughter, but time will tell. I hope it will not be necessary to discipline her again, but I shall not hesitate to do so if the need arises."

She regarded him, her gaze unwavering. Her response was slow in coming, and brief. "I see."

What did she see? Richard wondered. He felt a rare need to explain himself to this woman whose respect mattered to him. "England is under Tudor rule now. Castle Whitleigh must accept this and adjust, as must the rest of our country. I intend to do what I can to bring this about. I have been charged with bringing Castle Whitleigh to heel, and I mean to do just that, whatever it takes. A peaceful transition is preferable, which brings me to the purpose of my visit here. I would be honoured if you would join me and my men for the evening meal. It will do much to promote harmony if the de Whyttes are seen to break bread with the new Duke of Whitleigh."

"The conflict in our country has gone on for too long already as powerful men have fought over the crown, ripping and tearing at our families in their quest for power. If it is over, the matter settled, then I am glad of it. I have no desire to see hostilities prolonged, and certainly I do not wish to bring the conflict to my own doorstep. If you, and your new king, are able to bring all of us together to live in harmony, then I welcome that."

"So, you will sit beside me at tonight's table?"

"What of Frances?"

He allowed a wry smile to form. "I doubt if she will wish to join us in the main hall this evening and would struggle to be seated even if she did."

"I expect you are right."

"In the future, though, I hope that she will feel able to take her rightful place in this household once again."

"I see. I share your hope, my lord. I would be honoured to join you, and I do appreciate your reasons for inviting me. But I fear I must decline. I rarely come down for my meals these days. The stairs, you see…"

"Yet you managed to make it as far as the courtyard earlier."

"It cost me considerable effort, I assure you, but I felt it right that I should demonstrate solidarity with my granddaughter. I would not let her face you alone, though I fear I was of little use to her. I am afraid I rarely leave my room ordinarily."

He regarded the elderly dowager, took in the cluttered surroundings which clearly served as bedchamber, dining room, and sitting room. "It cannot be pleasant, to be isolated so in your own home."

"One of the pitfalls of living a long life, my lord. And preferable to the alternative."

"Please, use my given name. Richard."

She nodded. "Richard. And I am Margaret."

He extended his hand. "I hope we will be friends, Margaret. And I hope I may rely on your support in convincing the rest of this household to accept me as their new master."

The dowager smiled. "If you refer to my granddaughter, Richard, I suspect you will be able to accomplish that without my aid. She responds best to firmness, tempered with fairness and justice. If you are a good lord to her people, she will come to respect that."

"I thank you for your sound wisdom, and for your confidence, Margaret. As for the meal this evening, I will send men to assist you into the hall."

"In that case, I will thank you for your consideration. I believe I shall enjoy the company."

The meal was pleasant enough. The kitchens at Castle Whitleigh were clearly well-run and had adapted with quiet efficiency to the sudden demand to feed over a hundred men. Richard regarded the assembled throng, his own men, in the main, though a handful of villagers had responded to the invitation to attend the hall and eat with their new lord. He suspected the flavoursome, plentiful food was the main attraction after weeks of hardship, though some would no doubt be curious regarding his intentions.

They would learn soon enough. Hard work, honesty, obedience — these were qualities he admired and would reward. Provided they played their part in making Castle Whitleigh the prosperous estate he knew it could be, the local population had nothing to fear from him.

Lady Margaret had arrived on a converted chair, carried by two of his stoutest soldiers. He had instructed that carrying handles be attached to a solid carver chair, and seated upon this, the dowager had been carried down the stairs to join him in the hall. On the level, he noted that she was reasonably mobile. She walked with the aid of a stick but was perfectly able to get about. She greeted many of the servants by name, asking after their families, their health, and was clearly a popular figure here. She took her place at his side and made polite, if stilted, conversation with Stephen who sat on her other side.

He recognised the girl, Sara, when she trotted past bearing a pitcher of ale. She looked sprightly enough despite her ordeal, but he noticed she gave his brother a wide berth. Probably wise, he concluded.

Lady Margaret made her excuses after a couple of hours, and Richard permitted her to return to her room. She had done well.

All in all, his first day as master of Castle Whitleigh had been a success.

More or less.

The next morning, Richard was up and about soon after daybreak. He had installed himself in the lord's chamber and was pleased to find the accommodations spacious and comfortable, unlike his own ancestral keep. Whitleigh was very much to his liking, he concluded. He could put down roots here.

He descended into the hall again to find the servants already lighting the fires and bringing trays of bread and cheese up from the kitchens. The place was clearly efficiently managed, a credit to both Lady Margaret and Lady Frances. People knew their tasks and got on with them.

Neither of the de Whytte ladies was present now though. A plump, middle-aged woman appeared to be in charge, strutting about and barking orders at all within earshot. She rushed over as soon as she caught sight of him.

"My lord, I need tae speak wi' ye."

Richard sank into the lord's chair and reached for a piece of bread, still warm from the oven. "Oh?"

"We be needin' fresh vittals, my lord, what wi' ye an' yer bloody siegin'. Ye'll have tae send men out huntin'. I can cure pork, an' hang a nice side o' venison fer the winter, but I cannae go oot an' take the wee beasties doon meself."

He blinked. "What?" Her words sounded vaguely as though they might be English, but he could not be certain. "I beg your pardon."

"Meat," she repeated. "Ye need tae go huntin'."

He grasped most of that and saw the sense in what she was telling him, though he would have preferred to be allowed to break his fast before faced with the domestic realities of his new station in life. "Very well, I shall see to it."

"Mind ye do, lad." She turned and stomped off in the direction, he supposed, of the kitchens.

Lad?

Richard shook his head and managed not to chuckle.

He swung his gaze about the almost empty hall, taking in details which had eluded him yesterday. Several doors led off in various directions. The one at the end would take him outside, through the main entrance and out into the bailey, and the narrow opening beside the fireplace gave access to the spiral staircase leading up to the lord's solar. The main stairs, at the end opposite the entrance, rose to the first floor and the bedchambers occupied by himself and the two de Whytte ladies. Stephen had claimed another chamber for his own use so that corridor would be busy enough.

He could work out which was the door to the kitchens based on the bustling activity of the maids and serving lads, but that left just a couple unexplored. He got to his feet and strolled across the rushes strewn over the floor. The first door he tried turned out to be a storeroom, though its contents were somewhat depleted at present. The other door, on the opposite wall, swung open to reveal an ante-room, a place where visitors might wait until the lord was ready to see them. It was generously proportioned, and the window afforded a pleasant view across the moat and the open landscape beyond. Richard studied the ante-room, wondering if it was actually required for its intended purpose. He decided not, and in any case, he had a far better use in mind for it.

Back in the main hall, he stopped a passing servant. "I need a carpenter. Have him attend me here. Oh, and that woman who was here earlier, the one in charge of the kitchens…"

"You mean Mrs Lark, my lord?"

He nodded. He probably did. "Yes. Mrs Lark. Ask her to come and see me, too."

*****

She ached, even in places she never previously

realised she had. Every muscle, every joint, every bone in her body protested each time she tried to move.

Frances whimpered and attempted to sit up. She had to get out of bed or freeze to death. No one was likely to show up and light her fire, so she would have to do it herself, assuming that oaf masquerading as an earl had thought to have firewood sent up.

She was surprised to find that he had and was even more astonished to see that the fire had been laid, just waiting for her to put a light to it. She picked up a candle, lit it from a torch on the wall, then, moaning, she crouched to set fire to the kindling.

It was only as she eased herself painfully back to her feet that she remembered she was naked.

Dear Lord! Her face heated as she recalled not just the spanking she had endured, but the intimacies she had permitted afterwards.

What was I thinking? How could I...?

She crawled back into bed and buried her face under the pillow. How would she ever face him again? How would she face anyone?

She had had no choice about the spanking. Well, the alternative had been unthinkable, so surely that counted as no choice. He had insisted that she undress, so that, too, was not of her doing. But that final part, when he had held her and offered comfort — she had wanted that.

God forgive her, she had begged him to stay, not to leave her alone with her misery. And, he had done as she asked. She supposed he had stayed until she fell asleep as she had no recollection of him leaving.

In contrast, every horrendous moment of the spanking was indelibly etched upon her memory. She had never experienced pain like it, had been convinced she would expire, or at the very least be rendered senseless.

She emerged from beneath the pillow. It had been a moment of weakness and vulnerability. She had been scared, confused. Hurting. So, she had reached out to the one person who was there, who might understand how she felt since he had caused it.

Frances sighed. She was not in the habit of being untruthful, and certainly not with herself. Fear had not motivated her needy behaviour. She had been afraid before he spanked her, but not then, not after he said they were done. He was leaving, and she had stopped him. He was her enemy. Her family were ruined because of men like him, yet she had sought comfort from the Earl of Romsey, the one man she detested most in the world.

Her bout of self-loathing was interrupted by a knock at the door. Frances groaned and rolled onto her side. She was in no mood to see anyone.

The knock sounded again, and this time was accompanied by her grandmother's voice. "Frances? Can I come in, my darling?"

"Leave me be. Please." She just needed to be left alone.

The door opened. Her grandmother peered in.

"Did you not hear? I said—"

"I know what you said. I chose to ignore you, my dear." The dowager entered, balancing upon her stick. "Ah, I see you have a nice fire going. I have asked Mrs Lark to send up a tray."

"I am not hungry. So, please…"

Lady Margaret ignored Frances' churlish welcome, choosing instead to settle herself on the edge of the bed. "I came in to see you last night, after Richard left."

"Richard?"

"The earl. Or should we now refer to him as the duke?" She paused. "That will take some getting used to, I daresay. Anyway, his given name is Richard."

Frances scowled. "I had not realised your previous friendship extended to such familiarity." Her tone was decidedly frosty

"It did not, but we spoke. Last night. He is… quite personable once you get to know him."

"He is a brute." Frances muttered. "I hate him."

"Be that as it may, he tells me that the pair of you have arrived at an understanding."

"Since you were in here last night, you will surely appreciate why I felt compelled to accede to his demands."

"Quite so. I do understand. I have brought a salve with me which will help to ease your aches and pains this morning. Richard gave his permission. He has no wish to cause you further unnecessary discomposure."

"Aches and pains? Discomposure?" Frances glared at her grandmother. "That heavy-handed bastard actually took his belt to me…"

"I know, dear. I saw the marks. So, shall I apply the salve?"

"How can you be so calm about it? His belt, Grandmêre! Look." She drew the blankets back to reveal a portion of her hip, still glowing bright crimson from the earl's ministrations. "I shall be black and blue."

"Not if we rub some of this in quickly enough. It contains extract of apples, which will help, and a little aloe vera and parsley to reduce any swelling and soothe the discomfort. If you would lie on your stomach for a few moments, I shall smear it on."

"Just leave the pot," Frances snapped. "I shall do it myself. Later."

"Child, must I insist? Better still, I could summon Richard and ask him to talk some sense into you."

"You will do no such thing. If I am obliged to set eyes on that vile individual again, I shall—"

"Hush, now. You will have to learn to get along with him since he is here to stay. Castle Whitleigh may be a generously proportioned keep, but it is not that big that you might avoid him forever. And since you must face him, you may as well so do in relative comfort. Let me help you."

Faced with no better prospects, Frances rolled onto her stomach, then winced when her grandmother drew the blankets down to her ankles. "Is it very bad?" she whispered.

"You will live," Lady Margaret replied, "but I am sure Richard will have already told you that."

"Did he…? Is my skin broken? Do you think there will be scars?"

"No. No broken skin, and I am sure there will be no permanent marks. I suspect the earl knew what he was doing."

Frances could find no ready response to that. She cringed as her grandmother spread the salve across her still-heated skin, then massaged it in with fingers which were gentle but firm.

"My thighs are the most sore," she breathed. "He was especially harsh there."

"It is a tender area, and yes, there are some marks there, but most are on your bottom. They will heal, but I suggest you remain in your chamber for a day or so. Take your rest and let your body recover."

"I cannot. I must see to... things."

"What things? Mrs Lark has matters under control in the kitchens, and I can supervise the household."

"From your chamber? I hardly think so."

"Richard has ordered a chair be converted so that I can be safely carried downstairs. He has even allocated men to the task. I have but to ask and they will come to my aid."

"Oh." Frances was at a loss. Why had she not thought of such a solution? "So, you have been down to the hall?"

"I have, yes. Richard invited me to eat with him last night."

She glared at the elderly woman. "You did not agree, surely."

"I did, and it was most pleasant. Mrs Lark had prepared some duck. I suppose one of Richard's men must have shot it. And there are plenty of vegetables, now that the harvest has been brought in."

"But did you not hear what he did? To poor Sara?"

The dowager nodded. "That was most unkind, and I have had words with him on the matter. I do not believe such harsh measures to be typical of him."

"You had words with him?" Frances was incredulous.

"I did. If we are to make the best of this...
arrangement, I felt it imperative to be clear from the outset. I am satisfied with what I heard, and I believe it best now if we put the events of yesterday behind us. It is time to look to the future. Do you not agree?"

"The future? I dread the future, Grandmêre." She clutched at the dowager's sleeve. "Edmund is gone. We will never see him again. Our home is seized, snatched from under us. The Tudor rules England, the House of York has fallen…"

"Yet, here we are." The dowager's expression was stern. "We are both fit and well…" She eyed Frances' abused posterior. "…more or less. As are the rest of our household. Everyone is fed, all have a roof over their heads. It could have gone much worse for us."

"But—"

"We go forward, Frances, and we make the best of that which we cannot change." Lady Margaret eased herself to her feet, her movements stiff with age. "I shall leave you now. Remain here, if you must, for a day or so. Let yourself heal and think on what I have said. Then, when you are ready, come out and join the household again. We need you."

Chapter Six

Frances threw back the blankets and swung her legs out of bed. The soreness had gone, almost, and she could move about with ease. She could even sit in relative comfort, having spent most of yesterday perched on her window seat observing the goings-on in the courtyard below.

She had caught sight of the earl from time to time, striding here and there, issuing orders, she did not doubt. He would have everyone rushing about, in fear of their lives. The dark soldier who she understood to be his second-in-command was very much in evidence, too. The pair were frequently together, their heads bowed as they discussed some detail or other of their campaign to subdue Castle Whitleigh.

Her grandmother had not returned to pester her again, though the maids had been very much in evidence, flitting in and out with clean linens and piles of dry firewood. Mrs Lark sent up a tray of food three times a day, and Frances had to concede that their pantries must be well-stocked now. She had been served chicken, duck, fresh eggs, a few slices of succulent venison, and yesterday evening she had enjoyed a very fine portion of her favourite smoked salmon.

She could not, in good conscience, remain huddled in her chamber for yet another day. It was not fair to leave all the work to others. However much she preferred to avoid confronting that man again, she must shoulder her share of the duties.

Today, she would go down to the hall. She resolved to do so with her head high, and if anyone so much as mentioned her spanking, she would... well, she would cross that bridge when she came to it.

One of the maids, Molly, scuttled in with an armful of kindling. Frances waylaid the girl and requested her assistance in fastening her gown and arranging her hair. She chose her blue woollen dress, a plain and serviceable affair suited to supervising household chores or perhaps taking a turn about the village. There were calls she should make, people whose welfare she really ought to check on.

Molly managed to comb out her hair and braid it

neatly, though her fingers were not as deft as Sara's. Frances made a mental note to call on Sara's mother, who had been ailing of late. Betsy Tinker was the healer for the castle and surrounding village and much in demand. Apart from collecting and preparing herbs for her remedies, she had much else to occupy her, with her husband dead these last three years and a young son whose energy seemed boundless. And now, she had caught a chill and been confined to her bed for the last several days. Thank goodness Sara was still at home to assist.

Frances thanked Molly for her aid and dismissed the girl. She then spent a good few minutes with her palm on the door handle, steeling herself for the stresses of this, her first day as the usurped mistress of Castle Whitleigh.

She took a deep breath and stepped out into the flagged hallway. To her right lay the duke's chamber. She assumed that despicable brute of an earl would have claimed that for himself by now along with her brother's title. To her left was the room occupied by her grandmother. Certain of her welcome, Frances decided to start there. The dowager would no doubt have words of wisdom and encouragement to offer her. She approached the door and knocked.

There was no answering summons from within.

Frances frowned. Perhaps the dowager was sleeping. She knocked again, a little harder. There was still no answer, so she called out.

"Grandmère? It is me, Frances. May I come in?"

She was met with only silence. Even if the old lady had been asleep, she would have been roused from her slumbers by now. She never slept very deeply, and certainly not in the middle of the day.

Worried, Frances called out again. "Grandmère? Are you all right? May I come in?" This time, she did not wait for a reply. She grasped the doorknob and turned it. The door swung open.

Frances gasped, then stifled a scream. Wide-eyed, she took in the scene before her.

The room was deserted. Barely a stick of furniture remained. Her grandmother's bed was gone, as was her small table and the two chairs she liked to draw close to the fire. The grate itself was empty and cold. Even the hangings had been stripped from the walls, tapestries worked by Frances' great-grandmother and among the dowager's most treasured possessions.

Where are you? What have they done with you?

Fear churned her gut, and outrage. The cruel, callous bastard. It was bad enough that he had seen fit to lay his hands on her, but to oust an old lady from her chamber, take her things from her. This was heartless beyond measure, beyond imagining.

Was her grandmother well? Had they… hurt her?

Oh, dear sweet merciful Lord, please do not let it be…

Please, let them not have…
Why did no one even tell me?"

She could not bring herself to complete the thought. It was too awful, unthinkable.

Sobbing with rage and grief, Frances whirled on her heel and ran from the barren chamber. She would find the earl, and there would be a reckoning for this day's work.

She bolted down the main stairs, taking them two at a time, to emerge, panting, in the great hall. She scanned the huge chamber and saw him at once. The earl stood with his back to her, in conversation with two of his soldiers. The men were grinning, clearly enjoying a joke together.

At the expense of the poor, vanquished inhabitants of Castle Whitleigh, no doubt. Frances' temper soared.

She flew across the hall, letting out a furious screech as she neared him.

"You lying, treacherous bully. You vile bastard. Murderer!"

He turned a moment before she reached him, but not quickly enough to evade the small but determined fist aimed at his jaw. Encouraged by her early success, though not even remotely appeased, Frances continued to lay into him with fists and feet, and to regale him with every foul name and epithet she could call to mind.

"Blackguard! Bully! Liar!" she screamed, intent upon

pummelling him into submission.

Her attack was quickly halted when her quarry seized her wrists and swung her around so her back was to him, then quite simply wrapped his arms about her to force her to be still.

"What the holy fuck is this?" he demanded, when at last she ceased her name-calling. "A simple 'good morning' is more customary."

"Do not dare to make fun of me, you... you yaldson."

The earl stiffened at the insult, but Frances was unrepentant. She kicked at his shins, wrestling furiously in her attempts to escape the confining hug. "Let go of me, you lout. Do you mean to be rid of me as easily? Why not simply strangle me and be done with it?"

"I confess, I am sorely tempted," he growled into her ear. "But first, I prefer to know what has you so riled."

"Where is she? What did you do with her? Where are her belongings?"

"Who?"

"You know who. I just—"

"Frances, dear, is something amiss?"

Frances gaped. Wide-eyed, incredulous, she watched her grandmother emerge from the ante-room at the side of the hall. The elderly lady appeared almost as astonished as Frances at the scene before her.

"Has something happened?" the dowager asked, looking from her granddaughter to the earl who still held her firmly in his arms. "I heard shouting..."

"Grandmêre? Is it you?"

"Of course it is me, dear. Who else would it be?" The dowager eyed her curiously. "Are you quite all right, Frances? You appear somewhat... overwrought."

"I thought... I mean, I was sure that..."

"What did you think, dear?" the dowager enquired.

"Aye. Do tell us," the earl pressed her. "I am intrigued to know what brought on this temper tantrum."

Frances ignored him and addressed her response to Lady Margaret. "I went to your room, but it was empty. You

68

were gone. All your things were gone. I thought…"

"Ah, yes. Richard was kind enough to offer me the use of the old ante-room. He thought it might suit me better, since I would not need to worry about stairs so much. He had my furniture brought down here."

"The… the ante-room?" Frances repeated.

"Yes. It really is very cosy. And so convenient. I can come and go as I please now and not be a bother to anyone."

"You were never a bother," Frances protested

"No, but it is better to be independent, is it not? And now, I can spend more time here in the hall with the rest of the household. I had forgotten how much I missed the daily chatter."

"You are not hurt?" Frances stepped forward when the earl loosened his grip. "They… they did not force you to move?"

"Force me? Of course not. Richard showed me the room, which he had had cleared and cleaned in readiness, and asked if I might like to make use of it. Mrs Lark helped to make it nice and comfortable with all my own wall hangings, and some of the men carried my furniture down. I could not fit everything in, but I no longer need the chairs as I can come and sit out here, on the settle by the fire. It is a much better arrangement, truly."

"I…" Frances was lost for words. It had never occurred to her, not once, that there might be a more reasonable explanation. And why had she herself not thought to install her grandmother on the ground floor rather than leaving her more or less confined to her chamber? It was so obvious, now she thought of it. "I am sorry. I leapt to conclusions." She turned to meet the earl's angry gaze. "My apologies, my lord. It was a misunderstanding, that is all. Most unfortunate, but—"

"Unfortunate indeed," he agreed, "since it brought you tearing down into my hall like a woman possessed, to lay into me in front of half the household, screeching insults and even besmirching my mother's reputation."

"Y-your mother?"

"You referred to me as a yaldson, did you not? The

69

son of a whore?"

Frances had the grace to flush as he related the vile insult.

"Frances! Did you really say such a thing?" The dowager was clearly appalled. "You must apologise. At once."

"I have said I am sorry, but really, it was not entirely my fault. Someone should have told me." Even to her, the excuse sounded lame.

It was clear that neither her grandmother nor the earl was impressed either.

His visage was stern and uncompromising, and he idly rubbed at his jaw where her fist had connected. "I had thought that matters were clear between us following our last encounter, Lady Frances. It seems that I was wrong, and I shall have no option but to repeat the lesson. Perhaps a switch this time. Would that make a more lasting impression, do you think?"

She gasped and backed away from him. "No. You cannot. It was a mistake. I only—"

"A mistake, yes. But one I am not prepared to see repeated. I told you I would have respect in this house, most particularly from you since you set an example for the rest. I mean to—"

"Please, Richard, would you permit me to deal with this?" The dowager moved to position herself between them. "I will speak with Frances and ensure that she truly understands the need to show proper deference to the new lord."

He regarded the older woman under his lowered brows. "Lady Margaret, you are not to be held responsible for your granddaughter's conduct."

"I know. But… I believe I can be of some assistance in this matter. Please, on this occasion, I beg your forbearance. Allow me to speak with her. Alone."

The earl swung his gaze from Frances to Lady Margaret and back again. At last, he nodded. "Very well. On this one occasion we shall proceed as you wish. If you prefer to be alone, I suggest that the pair of you use your chamber,

Margaret." He offered the dowager a polite nod, spared a scathing glance for Frances, then turned on his heel to resume his interrupted conversation.

Abruptly dismissed, Frances stood rooted to the spot. Ashamed, embarrassed, feeling particularly silly, she prayed yet again for the earth to open and swallow her. The Almighty was seemingly not prepared to oblige her, so it was left to her grandmother to grasp her by the elbow and steer her across the hall and into the old ante-room. The dowager shut the door behind them, then balanced on her stick as she regarded her granddaughter.

"Grandmêre, I—"

"Be silent!" Lady Margaret rarely raised her voice, but she did so now. "You will be quiet, for once, and listen to me."

"But I was only—"

"Only what? Only trying to get yourself killed? Or beaten again? How would that help anyone?"

"I thought…"

"I know what you thought. Everyone knows. You thought Richard capable of cold-blooded murder."

"Well, is that not the case? He is a soldier. He has killed many on the battlefield."

"That is entirely different, and you know it. Here, as lord of Castle Whitleigh, he has shown himself to be a reasonable and just man, kind to the weak, and generous. He is making an effort, and you could at least try to do the same."

"Make an effort? Why would I—?"

"Because if you care so little for your own life, so be it. But regardless of how much you rant and rave and wish it were otherwise, Richard is here. He is staying, and he is in charge. He is now the Duke of Whitleigh, by royal decree. If you stir up resentment and rebellion, it will end in tragedy, and not only for you. Do not endanger your people, girl."

"I would never do that," Frances argued. "I care about them, as much as you do."

"Then heed me, and heed me well. Richard has made it absolutely clear that he will permit no one to challenge his authority, and that includes you. It is bad enough that we have

71

lost Edmund, but let us not incur further bloodshed. You will accept what has happened, and you will behave yourself."

"You should have told me that you were moving from your chamber. I should have—"

"Why should anyone tell you anything when you choose to sulk in your room for days on end?"

"I was hurt. He… he hurt me. You know that. You yourself told me to rest and recover."

"Aye, overnight. Or for a day, perhaps. But you chose to lock yourself away for the best part of half a week whilst the rest of us had to adjust to a new lord and set things to rights. Your people need to see you, to know that you are well and that they will be, too."

"I… I never…" Frances was close to tears. She could find no words to argue. Was this really what people thought of her? That she was a self-indulgent coward, hiding away in her chamber like a whipped puppy?

"I know you did not mean any such thing." Lady Margaret's tone gentled. "You would never abandon your people or your responsibilities. But, you must see how it looked. You need to do better, Frances, starting right now."

Frances nodded. "I know. I am sorry. I… I let you down. *I* should have brought you down here, given you this room. *I* should have made you a chair to get up and down the stairs. How could I have not realised…?"

"My darling, I have never doubted your love and affection, not for a moment. You have nothing to berate yourself for. And you know I love you, too. I would never have spoken to you thus if I did not care. I want the best for you, for all of us."

"I know, but it is so hard, after all that has happened."

"Hard, yes, but you must succeed. The alternative is…" She paused and shook her head. "I do not care to consider the alternative."

"I will. I promise." Frances sank onto the edge of the bed and lowered her face into her hands. "I must start by apologising. First, to you, then to him."

"I agree. And the matter will not improve for keeping.

72

I accept your apology, my darling, so do not waste further time on me. Go now, find Richard and convince him that you are truly contrite and will afford him the respect he demands from now on."

Frances shuddered. Grovelling was not in her nature, but it would seem she must do so anyway. She met her grandmother's anxious gaze. "Very well. I shall try. If… if he decides he still needs to take a switch to me, then I must accept that, too, I suppose."

"You will do what needs to be done, endure what you must. I have every confidence."

"Best get on with it, I suppose." Frances paused, her hand on the doorknob. "By the way, I love your new chamber."

The dowager smiled. "Aye, me, too."

He was not in the hall when she emerged from her grandmother's room. Frances looked about but could not see him. She summoned one of the maids.

"Where is Sir Richard?" she enquired.

The girl shrugged. "I do not know, my lady. He went outside…"

The stables, probably. Or perhaps he had business at the forge, or in the village. Frances pondered waiting for him to return but decided against it. She would lose her courage if she allowed this to fester.

He was not to be found in the bailey, so she made her way around the keep, checking the forge as she went. The earl was not there. The stables, then. She would enjoy a visit there in any case since she had not seen her own little mare for over a week. Athena was long overdue an outing, and Frances would enjoy a canter across the moors, assuming she was still permitted such liberties.

But that must wait. She had a more pressing priority right now.

His voice carried from the open door to the stables. Frances peered inside to spot the earl leaning on a stall, his linen shirt sleeves rolled to his elbows. He reached up to tug on the ears of his huge stallion, the beast he had ridden that first day when she had confronted him in the courtyard. Now he murmured softly to the animal, which actually appeared to be listening to him.

Her courage, such as it was, almost failed her. Frances contemplated slipping away and perhaps trying again later. She would take the time to rehearse her little speech, come up with something suitably convincing, and present it nicely. Her plans were dashed by Athena, who must have caught her scent on the air and set up an eager whinnying.

The earl turned, spotted Frances hovering in the doorway. "May I be of assistance, Lady Frances?"

"I… I wanted to talk to you. Just for a moment."

"Then do so." He propped a hip against the door of the stallion's stall and folded his arms. Athena stamped her hoof impatiently. He glanced at the delicate little palfrey, so insistent upon not being ignored. "You seem to be causing another commotion, Lady Frances. I assume the mare belongs to you."

"She does, yes." Frances entered and squeezed past him to reach Athena's stall. "She has been cooped up for too long and no doubt expects an apple. I usually bring her one."

"Try her with this." The earl plucked a carrot from a sack by his feet. "Trojan enjoys these."

She took the carrot and offered it to the mare. Athena sniffed, then accepted the crunchy vegetable. It seemed to pacify her, and she subsided into contented chewing.

"Your stallion is called Trojan, then?"

"Aye."

"My mare is Athena."

"We share a fondness for mythology, perhaps," he observed. "Though I do not suppose you sought me out to discuss the mysteries of ancient Greece."

She shook her head. "I… I want to apologise."

"I see." He waited, apparently not prepared to offer any assistance.

"I… I should never have spoken to you as I did. And I should not have hit you."

"You are referring, I daresay, to that 'little

74

misunderstanding' which caused you to screech at me like a banshee and attempt to pummel me into an early grave."

She nodded. "I… I deeply regret what happened, my lord."

He quirked his lip. "I believe the only thing you deeply regret is my presence in this house."

"No! I mean, yes, but…"

He closed the short distance between them and cupped her jaw in his hand. "Look at me, Lady Frances."

She raised her gaze to meet his. Did his eyes need to be quite so dark? So forbidding? And so warm?

"I will permit you to speak freely to me when we are alone. I prefer there to be honesty between us. But be aware, Frances, I will not tolerate unseemly displays such as that which we all witnessed earlier. I will not have you encouraging others to take issue with this new arrangement, nor with my claim to the title of Duke of Whitleigh. You must realise by now that I shall not hesitate to make my point in any manner I deem suitable. So, you will guard your tongue in public, or you will be punished for it. Do I make myself clear?"

She nodded. "Yes," she whispered. "I… I swear, I will never speak to you so again."

He held her gaze for several moments more, then, "I cannot make a window into your soul, and ultimately, it does not matter to me what you think. I am interested only in what you do, and what you say. You will be polite, and respectful. You will be obedient, and you will encourage others to follow your example. By way of helping to ensure your compliance, and to remind you of your promise, I will require you to visit the coppice by the river and cut several switches. You will trim them and keep them in your chamber, in a pail of water, ready for my use should you forget yourself or encounter another such 'misunderstanding'." His grip on her jaw tightened. "Be under no illusion, Frances, it would take very little provocation to persuade me to bare your bottom again and apply a switch to it. The pain will be quite exquisite, I promise you, and it is an experience you will not wish to repeat."

She wondered if her knees were about to give way.

"There will be no need for that. I know what I must do, what you expect."

"You will collect the switches, though, and if they become decayed you will replace them with fresh ones. If I decide you would benefit from a switching, I will expect them to come readily to hand."

"I… yes. I understand."

"I am relieved to hear it, not least as I hold Lady Margaret in high regard, and she will be most upset if there is discord between us."

"She speaks highly of you, too. And… it was considerate of you to offer her the room next to the hall."

"I want her to be very much at the heart of this household. She is a good influence, on you, especially."

"You make it sound as though your kindness to her is self-serving."

"You think otherwise?" He raised an eyebrow. "Could it be that you are warming to me, just a little?"

"I will allow credit where it is due. I love my grandmother, and you have made her happy."

"I see. So, tell me, Frances, is your posterior quite recovered from our last encounter?"

"My…" She flushed but did not look away. "Yes. I am well, thank you."

"Well enough to enjoy an hour in the saddle?"

"In the saddle," she parroted. "You mean, I may go riding?"

"Trojan, too, would benefit from a canter. And I am keen to get to know the local area. I hope you will agree to act as my guide. You could introduce me to anyone we might meet, and it will be helpful for us to be seen in one another's company."

"So, it is about appearances."

He slanted her a glance she could not entirely interpret, though her heart did an odd little fluttery thing and warmth curled deep in her belly. "Not entirely. We might even enjoy the outing. So? Will you join me?"

Chapter Seven

Richard lounged in his solar, his booted feet resting on the table before him and a mug of ale to hand. His ride with Frances three days previously had gone well. She had turned out to be a pleasant and interesting companion and had even managed to make him chuckle once or twice with her ready wit and insightful comments regarding the people they encountered. He might even come to like the lass, given time.

And why not? Richard enjoyed the company of women and never lacked for female company. He was one of England's most sought-after and marriageable lords so there was never any shortage of noble families keen to dangle their daughters before him. He enjoyed the occasional dalliance and rarely wanted for females to share his bed. It never ceased to amaze Richard how wanton even the most gently raised young lady might become when she got a sniff of a wealthy and powerful husband.

Thus far, he had not been drawn into any protracted negotiations and was not on the lookout for a countess — or, indeed, a duchess — to share his life. Soldiering and domesticity did not make happy bedfellows, in Richard's opinion. With these thoughts in mind, he reread the letter hand-delivered to him an hour earlier. Even now, the courier waited in the guardroom, having been instructed to return with the earl's response.

Richard recognised the king's own handwriting, and the ornate royal seal. There could be no doubt as to the authenticity of the letter, and on reflection, Richard could not really take issue with the contents. If nothing else, Henry Tudor could never be accused of failing to lead by example.

The missive confirmed the plans which all had known of but were now in hand. The king was to wed, and his chosen bride was none other than Elisabeth of York, the daughter of King Edward, the fourth of that name, and the niece of Richard who had lost his crown to Henry Tudor at Bosworth. The tactics were obvious. The king meant to keep his friends close and his enemies closer. By uniting the houses of York and Lancaster he could reduce the likelihood of further challenges for the crown. Edward IV's grandchildren would inherit the throne through their mother. There would be no need to fight for it.

It was brilliant in its simplicity. Added to which, Elisabeth was an acclaimed beauty. The king could do worse. Far worse.

The letter included Richard's invitation to attend the nuptials which were to take place in just under three months' time. But that was not all. Henry expected his loyal supporters to follow his example and take brides who could help to cement the new regime. He would not command Richard to marry, their friendship ran too deep for that, but the king's wishes were plain. Richard was expected to wed a woman of the house of York, if he chose to marry at all. Henry was asking nicely, but he was still asking.

The missive also made reference to the 'problem' of the residual members of the de Whytte family. It irked Henry that Edmund de Whytte had eluded justice, and he queried the loyalties of Lady Frances and Lady Margaret. The dowager was probably safe enough since she was unlikely to present any serious challenge, and Richard would gladly vouch for her. However, it had not escaped Henry's attention that Edmund de Whytte had left behind a sister, of marriageable and child-bearing age. As far as the king was concerned, Lady Frances de Whytte was biding her time, just waiting to bring forth a horde of hostile little Yorkists ready to perpetuate the war between the royal cousins. This was not to be permitted. The king required the girl to be dealt with.

Richard was charged with settling the matter as he thought fit, though the king personally recommended sealing the inconvenient young woman away in a convent where she was unlikely to breed. Twenty years or so should be sufficient, then she might emerge to do as she liked.

Richard took a generous slug of his ale. A less convincing nun he had yet to meet. Frances would be distraught, and he found himself caught between a rock and a hard place. He had promised her that she could enjoy her freedom in exchange for her good behaviour. She had complied. He had no complaints. Well, not really. The girl was stubborn, but she was no fool. She made the occasional barbed comment still but had the sense to only do so in private. They had learned to get along, and he was reluctant to break his side of the bargain.

He rolled up the parchment and sent word to the guardroom that he would not be replying at once and the king's messenger should make himself comfortable.

Richard stalked from the solar. He needed fresh air, time to think, to consider his options. Stephen was in the courtyard and raised his arm in greeting as Richard strode in the direction of the stables.

He waved back, barely breaking his stride. A gallop on Trojan would help to clear his thoughts. He had started to saddle the stallion when Stephen joined him in the stable.

"Brother, is something amiss?"

Richard cast a glance his way. "Aye, you could say that. Henry is minded to banish Lady Frances to a nunnery."

Stephen whistled between his teeth. "That would be a waste," he observed. "Does she know of this?"

"What do you think? Are the rafters still intact? Is she screaming to the heavens?"

"No, then." Stephen lifted his saddle from the rack and strode toward his own warhorse. "I assume we are going somewhere."

"There is no need for you to come. I simply fancied a ride. I need to think."

Stephen did not answer, but the pair cantered across the courtyard together and crossed the drawbridge side by side. Once beyond the confines of the keep and its walls, they dug in their heels, and the mighty horses sprang forward.

Half an hour later, and perhaps ten miles from the Whitleigh, they reined in their mounts. The stallions panted, then, content that they had expended their pent-up energy, they lowered their heads to chomp at the hedgerow. Richard slid from Trojan's back and slung the reins around a tree stump. If only his own dilemma could be solved so easily.

Stephen dismounted, too, and the pair ambled down a bank to the edge of the river. They crouched, scooped up water in their hands, and drank. Then Stephen turned to regard his brother.

"So, what do you mean to do about her, then? And why is Henry so set on this madness?"

Richard outlined the logic. "His Majesty is seeking to unite his turbulent nation. He is to wed a woman of the York house, and he wishes the rest of us who are not already married to do likewise."

"I can see that would be a decent strategy, and not such a misfortune. The Yorks have bred some fine women, from what I have seen."

Richard did not disagree.

"But what does this have to do with Lady Frances taking the veil?"

"The king will not permit her and others like her, women of the house of York, to wed Yorkist men and restore their shattered families over the next several generations. He prefers to bury such females in the cloister until they are no longer of child-bearing age."

"I can see the logic in that. 'Twould be a shame, though."

"Aye." Richard shook his head. "She will never accept this. We have, up to now, managed to arrive at some sort of uneasy truce, she and I. But that will be shattered. She will be convinced that I have betrayed her if I deliver her into the clutches of a convent."

"You cannot resist the king's command."

Richard shook his head. "I cannot. But, there is an alternative."

"There is, certainly. So, you have considered that prospect, then?"

Richard was glad of the need to elaborate no further. "Aye," he replied. "I have."

"And?"

"I have no desire to be wed. You know that."

"Especially not to a belligerent young woman who loathes you."

"She does not loathe me. I think…"

Stephen shrugged. "Perhaps not, though on occasion she has created a damned fine impression of it. Despite her hostility, though, she is a comely lass. She would not be a hardship to bed. If you do not want her, I believe I might offer…"

Richard whirled around to grasp his brother by the front of his shirt. "You will keep your hands off her."

Stephen grinned at him, unimpressed by the show of temper. "Will I? Then you must get to her first, my brother."

Richard's response was a non-committal grunt. He released Stephen's shirt and got to his feet. "We ought to be getting back."

Their return journey was more leisurely. They kept to a gentle canter, following the route of the River Tavy, and slowed to a walk when the castle came into view.

Stephen shielded his eyes to take in the vista. "It is a pretty spot," he observed. "And secure. Well-fortified. You mean to stay here, I assume."

"Aye, I think so."

"What of Keeterly Castle?"

Richard had not been back to his family seat for over five years. His duties as one of Henry's foremost warlords had kept him on the move, and that had suited him well enough. Until now, he had felt no pressing urge to settle, though of late he had become tired of campaigning and ready for fresh challenges. The ancient Parnell keep north of Exeter was larger than Castle Whitleigh, but it was nowhere near as comfortable. He slanted a glance at his brother. "I had thought you might like to have Keeterly."

Stephen shot him a look. "You are the earl, not me."

"We share the same father. Everyone knows that. He acknowledged you, and you are his eldest son. The king could convey the title to you, and I believe he would do so if I were to ask it of him."

"Why would you do that? Apart from anything else, the title is your birthright. You are legitimate. I am not."

Richard shrugged. "I am not interested in that, or in Keeterly. Would you take the earldom if it was offered?"

"Aye. Gladly. Keeterly was my childhood home as

well as yours."

"I will send word to Henry."

"If you also send him word of your forthcoming marriage to the lovely Lady Frances, I believe he would do anything you asked of him."

Richard grinned. "We shall see. I doubt if Frances—"

His words were cut off by a high-pitched shriek from behind them. Both men whirled their horses around to face the danger.

"Is that…?"

"'Tis Sara," Stephen confirmed. "The lass I scared half to death the day we arrived here."

"Well, something else has terrified her now."

The girl was running towards them as hard as she could, skirts and hair flying, screaming at the top of her lungs. "Save him, Please… Donald, my brother…"

"What the…?" Stephen stood up in his stirrups to gain a better view of whatever was amiss. "I cannot see anything."

A movement caught Richard's eye, a brief flash of brown in the river behind the girl. He screwed up his eyes and stared at the fast-flowing stream then let out a shout. "In the water. Look."

Stephen swore. "God's bones! It's a lad, he must have fallen in."

They moved as one, kicking their horses into a gallop and racing along the meadow, keeping a course parallel to the river.

Richard bent low over his mount's neck for extra speed and offered up thanks that the weather of late had been relatively dry and the river was not flowing as fast as it might. "We need to be downstream," he yelled, nudging his stallion closer to the stream. "We have to get ahead of him. You take the bridge."

Stephen nodded and continued straight ahead, when Richard nudged his horse to gallop along the water's edge. He kept up the breakneck pace until he was several yards ahead of the small, tousled head bobbing the water. He considered

galloping Trojan right out into the flow but decided against it and instead launched himself from the animal's back to land in the river. He was downstream of the boy –
Donald, had the girl said? – and had but to get a hold of him as he was swept past.

Several powerful strokes brought Richard out into the middle of the river. He could see the Donald's terrified expression now, his small hands reaching for something, anything.

Richard grabbed at him and missed. He spun around and launched himself after the boy, and this time succeeded in clutching a hadful of his trailing cloak. He caught one of the Donald's flailing arms and pulled him to his chest.

"Be still, lad," he murmured. "I have you."

Richard looked over his shoulder. Had Stephen reached the footbridge?

Thank the dear Lord. Stephen was perched on the edge of the bridge and already tossing a rope into the current. The other end was securely attached to his stallion's saddle. All Richard needed to do was get hold of the rope as the river carried him and young Donald under the bridge. He kicked his feet to gain a better position in the water and hung on to the thin body in his arms. The child could not be more than six or seven years old, he thought. Too young to die.

This time his aim was truer, and he seized the rope at the first — and probably only — attempt. He wound it around his wrist and grunted when his arm was almost yanked from its socket. They came to a juddering stop just under the bridge.

Stephen lay on the bridge, both hands extended. "Let me take him."

The water was chest deep, and now that he was no longer being swept downstream, Richard was able to get a solid footing and stand upright to lift Donald from the current. He heaved the lad up high enough for Stephen to grasp his arms and haul him onto the bridge. Then Stephen reached down again, and this time clamped his fist around Richard's free hand. Moments later, he, too, lay gasping and dripping wet on the narrow footbridge.

"Is he all right?" Richard coughed. "Did we get to

him in time?"

Stephen nodded. "Looks like it.

Beside them, the boy also coughed water from his lungs. Stephen pulled him into a sit and thumped him between the shoulder blades. Donald leaned forward and promptly vomited, then he turned his tearful gaze on his rescuers. "I lost my fishing pole," he complained.

They were about halfway back to the castle when Sara reached them, panting for air. Richard and Stephen were on foot, leading their stallions. The boy sat astride Trojan and appeared to be thoroughly enjoying his adventure now that the peril was averted.

"Thank you, thank you," she gasped, her face flushed from running. "You saved him."

"Aye, we—"

Sara flung her arms around a startled Richard. "I thought he was lost, for sure. If you had not been there..."

"Well, we were. And all is well. Or it will be as soon as he is warm and dry and furnished with a new fishing pole. So, you may unhand me, if you would..."

The girl released him and hung her head. "I apologise. I should not have..."

"Well, my brother may not appreciate the familiarity, but you can always hug me if you like." Stephen grinned at her.

Sara reddened. "My lord, I... I..."

"I trust you do not fear me still," Stephen prompted.

"Of course not. You helped to save my brother. You are very nice, and very handsome. And... And..." She floundered, clearly wishing she had never started this.

"'Tis a fair walk to the castle. Would you like a ride back, Sara?" Richard decided to take pity on the embarrassed maid.

"Sir?" She regarded the horses with undisguised suspicion.

"Your mount is taken, brother. Sara shall have the use of mine." Stephen beckoned her to him and led her around to the side of his warhorse. "Your foot?" He linked his hands to form a step and boosted the girl up into the saddle. She shrieked in fear but took only a few moments to settle herself.

Richard cast an assessing look his brother's way, then resumed their leisurely pace.

He needed to speak with Lady Frances. It was not a prospect he especially relished.

*****

Frances had witnessed the rescue from her window in the keep. She heard the frantic cries from outside and leaned out over the sill. She had observed the unfolding of events with her heart in her mouth and she had entertained scant hope that the earl and his brother would reach poor Donald before he was swept out to sea.

But they did. She had seen the earl launch himself into the water and had watched in astonishment as he managed to grab the drowning child. Only when all three of them were at last safe on the bridge, she let out a breath she had not even realised she was holding

She supposed the lad must be Sara's smaller brother, Donald, though she could not be sure from this distance. The boy was a lovable little rogue, always in some sort of bother. He had lacked for suitable male authority since the death of his father, a fisherman, three years ago. Sara and her widowed mother did their best, but young Donald had developed a tendency to run wild. She really must try to do something about the situation before it truly did end in tragedy.

She was at the drawbridge ready to meet the returning party, having already instructed servants to prepare a hot bath for the earl. She had also sent for Betsy Tinker, who lived in a small cottage in the village and may not have been aware of her son's brush with near disaster.

"That was well done, my lord," she said as soon as he was within earshot. "You, too, Sir Stephen. We are indebted to you."

Richard halted before her and reached up to assist the dripping wet boy from the saddle. "He needs dry clothing. And I gather he has lost his fishing pole."

"There will be no more fishing, not for him." The distraught mother rushed over to hug her son. "Donald, what were you doing? You know you're not allowed to go near the river on your own."

"I w-was not a-alone." The lad's teeth were chattering now. "S-Sara was there."

"Only because I was already by the river, washing some linens, and…" She accepted Stephen's assistance in dismounting, then clapped her hands over her mouth. "Oh, my lady, I forgot all about the sheets. I saw Donald fall in and I tried to reach out for him, but he was swept past me in a moment. I didn't know what to do, so I just set off running back here for help and I clean forgot. I left everything there, on the riverbank. I must just go and get them… "

Frances was having none of it. "The linens can wait, Sara. I am sure your mother will need your assistance. Do you have a bathtub in your cottage? And hot water?"

"Aye, my lady. We do. But—"

"I will see to the matter of the linens." Stephen leaned against his horse, his arms folded. "I believe I owe you that, at least, Sara, after my ill treatment when first we met."

"My lord?" Sara could not have looked more astonished, Frances thought, had the dark-haired knight sprouted wings and fluttered about her ancestral turrets. Indeed, she shared the girl's surprise.

"Go," Stephen insisted. "Go with your family."

Sara needed no more persuasion. She grasped Donald's hand firmly and marched him off in the direction of the village. Her mother followed, muttering dark threats which seemed to suggest that Donald would be growing whiskers before he might expect to be let out alone again.

Frances turned her attention back to the earl. "My lord, I cannot thank you enough. He is a headstrong lad but dearly loved…"

"It was nothing," he replied. "Stephen and I were close enough to help."

"But you risked your life. For us. Our people."

"Our people?" He paused and swung around to meet

her gaze. "Surely you mean my people."

"Of course, yes. But—"

"I am Duke of Whitleigh now, as I believe we have discussed before, at some length. The people of this estate are my responsibility. I will protect them, care for them, lead them, dispense justice to them. I take my responsibilities seriously, Lady Frances, and those responsibilities run to pulling unfortunate boys out of the river if need be. That child..." he jerked his thumb in the direction taken by Sara and her family, "that child is mine every bit as much as he is yours. I will thank you not to forget that, but if you require reminding again, I trust you have switches at the ready."

"My lord, I did not mean..." She paused, stricken. "I am sorry. Truly. Forgive me."

He furrowed his brow. "You know, for once, I actually believe you." He turned to make his way back into the house, then stopped again to scowl at her. "For Christ's sake, after all these weeks can you not bring yourself to call me by my given name?"

Chapter Eight

"Thank you for joining me so promptly."

Frances halted in the doorway of the lord's solar. The room was rarely used as the hall was more convenient. Richard's summons bringing her here suggested the need for privacy. Her curiosity was piqued, and she had wasted no time in hurrying up the barrow spiral staircase to find out what he wanted to discuss.

"I trust there is nothing amiss, my lo— Richard."

"Please sit down." He gestured to a chair opposite him. He was seated at a polished mahogany table, an item much cherished by her mother in the past. A sheet of parchment lay open before him. He waited until she was comfortable, her skirts neatly arranged, then raised one auburn eyebrow. "Can you read, Frances?"

She bristled. "Of course I can." Well, she could, more or less. She had never been especially adept at her letters but could generally get by.

He inclined his chin. "I have received a letter, from King Henry. It concerns you." He shoved it across the table towards her. "Please, read."

"Me?" Frances was baffled. "Why would the Tudor be concerned with me?"

"Just read." He settled back in his chair. "If you require me to explain anything, please ask."

Frances stared at the parchment. The looping script was small and closely written. She could pick out a few words, but it would take her a while to thoroughly read and comprehend the king's message.

"I… I…" She nibbled on her lower lip.

"Would you prefer me to read it to you?" he offered. "After all, I have had more time than you in which to study the contents."

"If you would. Thank you." Relieved at being able to retain her dignity, she folded her hands in her lap and waited for matters to be made clear.

Richard drew the parchment over to his side of the

table and started to read.

Frances had been aware of the king's marriage plans so was not surprised to learn of those. She interrupted Richard to ask if he intended to attend the wedding.

"Of course. It is the king," he replied.

"Yes. I suppose you must. Please, continue."

She could not entirely comprehend the mix of emotions which coursed through her when he reached the part where the king was clearly urging Richard to take a bride. It was not solely that such a match would bring a new mistress to Castle Whitleigh, though that was a poor enough prospect. She found the idea of a new duchess taking her place at Richard's side extremely unpalatable for reasons she was not quite prepared to examine.

It was only when he arrived at the section which set out the king's views on her own future that she leapt to her feet with a cry of "Never! I shall die first."

Richard set the parchment aside and regarded her silently. He was calm, unnaturally so.

"You. You knew of this."

"Of course. I received the letter yesterday and have had an opportunity to consider the king's suggestions."

"Did you put him up to this? How would he even know about me unless you told him?" Her temper surged. Despite all her best intentions and supreme efforts of recent weeks, she was as close to hitting Richard as she had been the day he had first marched into her home.

"Henry makes it his business to know of such matters. He perceives all Yorkists as a potential threat to his throne."

"But this is outrageous. He cannot do this. I will never agree."

"He is the king. Henry does not require your agreement."

"You promised me. You said…" She glared at him. "You said that if I accepted your punishment, and did not cause disruption here, then I would have my freedom. I would be allowed to remain at Whitleigh. I have done as we agreed."

"I know that, Frances, and I would be prepared to tell Henry as much. Certainly, I am confident that he will accept my guarantee that your grandmother need not be considered a threat."

"But not me? Why? Why does he believe me to be dangerous?"

"You know why. It is clear in his letter."

"He thinks I will bear sons who would rise up against him."

"That does seem to be the gist of it, yes."

"But, if I was to swear I would not wed without his consent, would that not suffice?"

"As a member of the English aristocracy with no male relative to manage your affairs, you already require royal consent to marry."

"Well, then…"

"Henry is well aware of the claims often made by illegitimate sons. The king himself has a somewhat dubious lineage, and see what he has made of it."

"Illegitimate? I would never…"

Richard shrugged. "Perhaps not. But Henry is nothing if not thorough."

Frances subsided back into the seat she had vacated moments before. The enormity of her predicament was beginning to sink in. In a fit of frustrated impotence, she covered her face with her hands and let out a shriek. "I hate him! I loathe all Tudors. Why can they not leave us be?"

"Frances, have a care. You must not be heard to speak against His Majesty. If you thought your situation dire now, be assured, it could become much, much worse."

"How could it become worse? I am to be packed off to some frigid cloister to waste away my days in prayer and self-deprivation. This king of yours intends to condemn me to a living death."

"There are many who do not consider a life of devotion to be such a dreadful fate. And you could select your preferred religious house."

She shook her head. "No. I will not do it. He cannot force this on me."

Richard got to his feet and came around the table to

envelop her in his arms.

Frances' first instinct was to shove him away. Was he not one of these hateful Tudors also, or an apologist for them? Richard resisted her futile efforts, so she surrendered to her second impulse which was to clutch his tunic and weep.

Richard continued to hold her, and even succeeded in manoeuvring her around so she found herself in his lap, sobbing against his chest. Why was it that her lowest moments, she seemed to end up here? She had no idea how long she remained in Richard's embrace giving vent to her grief and fury, but eventually she had no option but to raise her tear-streaked face and look him in the eye.

"You must think me a fool. An emotional idiot."

"No, I do not. I consider you badly served, in fact. None of this is fair."

"Yet, here we are." She sniffled. "What am I to do? I cannot leave my grandmother. I cannot bear to be forced from my home. I would die, I know it."

"There is another solution."

She gulped back her sobs. "What solution? What can I do?"

"You could wed, with the king's permission. Allow His Majesty to direct your choice of husband and all would be well."

She gave an unladylike snort. "What sort of addle-pated solution is that? I would find myself the bride of some elderly lecher, forced to go and rot in some distant keep and bear little Tudor babies."

"Not necessarily." He tipped her chin up so that she could not look away. "You could marry me."

Frances gaped at him, convinced she had misheard. "I… I beg your pardon."

"I said," he enunciated slowly, for the avoidance of any doubt, "that you could marry me."

"But you do not love me," she blurted. "You do not even like me."

His mouth curled in a warm smile. "Where did you get such a notion? I do like you. Well, most of the time."

"But we are not suited. You are a Lancastrian, and

91

I…"

"That is precisely why it is a good idea. The king desires me to take a Yorkist bride, and he insists that you must marry a Lancastrian or suffer the consequences. We have the perfect solution. It has the added benefit that you would not be compelled to move halfway across the country, and I trust you would not consider me too decrepit or lecherous for your taste."

"But, I do not… I mean, I have never…" She shook her head in bewilderment. "Why would you do this? You do not wish to wed."

"I have no objection to the married state, and I can imagine worse brides than you."

"Worse brides than me?" She was perversely affronted, despite having rejected his suggestion out of hand mere moments before. "That is a poor excuse for a proposal, sir."

"I agree. Allow me to rephrase it. Lady Frances de Whytte, will you be my bride? Please."

"But… why? You do not have to do this, you just said as much."

"I do not have to do this *now*, that is true. But I must marry at some stage. Castle Whitleigh needs heirs, and a duchess. It will fall to me to provide both, and I cannot imagine that a better candidate for the role of duchess is likely to emerge. And whilst there appears to be little in the way of unrest here at the Whitleigh, I cannot fault the king's personal strategy for uniting his divided nation. A marriage between you and I would be popular with the local people. More to the point, it would settle the future of the dukedom and make any subsequent challenge less likely. It makes perfect sense."

"I do not know what to say. I…"

"Then say nothing, for now. Take a few days to consider your options, stark though they are. Henry will wait, though sadly, not forever. His messenger is ensconced in our guardroom awaiting a reply to the king's letter, but as long as we keep the man well fed and comfortable, I believe we can delay matters for a while."

"I see." The dowager set aside her embroidery and tilted her head to one side to better regard her flustered granddaughter. Frances had wasted no time in rushing to find the dowager to seek her counsel. "A proposal of marriage? From Richard? Well, this is a turn-up, though I suppose it was to be expected. It is the perfect solution, after all. I trust you were suitably polite."

It struck Frances that her grandmother's assessment of the idea was almost exactly the same as Richard's. "I… I believe I was polite. Though I confess he took me by surprise."

"So, when is the wedding to take place?"

"I did not agree to marry him."

The dowager raised an eyebrow. "Whyever not?"

"Because… well, is it not obvious?"

"Not to me, my dear. Please, indulge me with an explanation."

"He is our enemy." Frances stared at her grandmother. For such a keenly intelligent woman, why did the dowager seem not to grasp that which was so glaringly obvious. "I cannot wed the man who usurped my brother."

"Richard is not *my* enemy, Frances. Neither is he the enemy of Betsy Tinker and that accident-prone son of hers. I do not believe anyone at Castle Whitleigh considers Richard to be anything other than a good and just lord."

"But what of Edmund?" Frances persisted

"We cannot turn back time. Edmund is gone. Your future is at stake, and what Richard has offered you is a fine prospect indeed. Infinitely better than a lifetime on your knees in a cold chapel. You would be Duchess of Whitleigh, assured of a life here with a good man who you can rely on to protect you."

Frances regarded her grandmother balefully. "Is this not the point at which you should be tutting and declaring that he is not even close to being good enough for me?"

The dowager smiled. "Well, naturally he is not, but we should try to overlook that failing."

"He does not love me. He only even likes me some of the time."

"He said that?" Lady Margaret's eyebrows shot up.

"Yes. Exactly that." Frances was adamant. "And… you know yourself that he spanked me. As his wife, he would consider it his right to do so again. And again. Whenever he saw fit."

"I daresay he would, should you give him cause. And as long as he is lord here and you remain under this roof, he will have that right whether you are his wife or not."

"But… he does not love me," she repeated. "I always imagined that when I wed, it will be to a man who adores me and who I can love in return."

Lady Margaret's stern expression relaxed into a sad smile. "A fine ideal. I applaud your ambition. But Frances, if Richard's love matters to you, then earn it."

"That is impossible. I cannot make him love me any more than I can make myself love him."

"Of course you can, on both counts. And I strongly suggest you get on with doing so." Lady Margaret picked up her embroidery again. "Now, since we have that settled, would you be so kind as to fetch me some more of this emerald-green thread from my chamber, dear?"

Her choice was made. Or rather, she had decided to settle for the lesser of two evils. Frances did not for a moment believe that she could achieve what her grandmother had suggested, but she did concede that it would be madness to reject the lifeline offered.

She had lost too much already — her brother, her position in society, her home. She had been forced to accept the humbling circumstances she now found herself in and had forged a way to cope. Life was far from ideal, but, as her grandmother was fond of pointing out, infinitely better than the alternative. Richard would make a challenging husband, but he was handsome, and not especially old. Thirty summers, perhaps, ten years her senior.

And… he had the power to arouse her. There had been occasions, more frequent of late, when he smiled at her in that lop sided manner he had and something odd happened deep in her core. She had even, on occasion, noticed a curious wetness in her most intimate places and she could not deny that he was probably the most handsome man of her acquaintance. Surely those were positive traits in a husband.

Yes, there were plenty of women who would envy her.

Frances willed the inconvenient flush to subside before she went in search of the man to tell him her answer. It would not do to let him know how powerfully he could affect her as he would surely take advantage.

There was no sign of Richard in the hall, but his brother was there, deep in conversation with Sara Tinker. Frances approached the pair.

Sara dropped a quick curtsey, and Stephen offered her a bow. "Can I help you, my lady?"

"I was hoping to speak with the earl. I mean, the duke." She swallowed hard. This was the first time she had freely acknowledged his rank. "Do you know where I might find him?"

"He is in the stables, my lady. Would you like me to send word that you seek him?"

She shook her head. "I will go and find him, thank you." She paused to select two juicy red apples from the bowl on the high table, and thus equipped, she set forth for the stable.

She popped her head around the door to find Richard grooming Trojan. The pearl-grey stallion gleamed under his master's ministrations and stamped his huge hooves on the cobbled floor. He raised his head when she entered and let out an interested snort.

Richard straightened and nodded to her. "Trojan appears pleased to see you, but I suggest you stay back. He can be unpredictable."

"I brought him an apple." Frances produced the fruit from her pocket. "And one for Athena, too."

"Ah, well, that accounts for your welcome, then."

"Will he bite me if I give it to him?"

"He is unpredictable but not a fool. Come forward a little. Stand beside me but stay on that side of the door."

She did as he advised, then held out her hand, flat, with the apple balancing on her palm. The warhorse nudged her fingers with his muzzle, which Frances decided was remarkably soft, given the ferocity of the animal. Then, the horse drew back his lips to reveal monstrous teeth, and gently removed the fruit from her hand. He took the offering and she felt nothing more than the flutters of his breath.

"Oh. He is quite tame, really," she exclaimed.

"I would not say that. But he does manage half-decent manners a lot of the time and he is always amenable to bribery. I suggest you keep the gifts coming if you truly wish to win him over."

Would that a handful of apples would achieve the same for you.

Frances swallowed painfully. "I… I have arrived at a decision, my lord."

He arched an eyebrow. "And?"

"And… I will accept your offer of marriage. That is, if you have not changed your mind."

"I have not. And I am delighted to hear it. I will send word to the king at once. May I leave the wedding arrangements in your hands, Frances?"

"Yes. Yes, of course." Frances resolved to keep the celebrations simple. She had not the slightest notion how to organise a wedding, but perhaps her grandmother would know. Or even Mrs Lark. "I… that is all. I just felt I should inform you immediately."

"I appreciate your consideration." He patted the stallion and exited the stall, then bent to rinse his hands in the bucket of water kept in readiness for such use. "There only remains, then, the matter of sealing our bargain."

"S-sealing our bargain? What do you mean?"

"I mean this, Frances." He placed his still damp hands upon her shoulders and drew her to him.

He smelled of straw and musk, and of leather. The odour reminded her of the occasion she had become closely acquainted with his belt, and she was dismayed to find the recollection strangely sensuous. Dampness gathered between her thighs. She tilted her head back to look up at him. Had his eyes always been so dark, the colour of rich, polished oak?

"Richard…?"

"Frances." He lowered his head to brush his lips over hers. "You taste sweet."

"I… I…"

He stopped her stammering by the simple expedient of covering her mouth with his own.

Frances was stunned. Her first impulse was to push against him, to break the kiss. It was too soon, too intimate. Even if she had tried, she would have failed. He did not want the kiss to end, and God help her, neither did she.

Instead of fighting as any decent woman should, she leaned into him and lifted her arms to wrap them around his neck. His hair curled around her fingers, silky, as she had imagined. She combed her fingers through the strands, then, in response to his insistent nibbling, she parted her lips to permit his tongue to enter.

Arousal surged. Waves of sensation which she could only describe as lust filled her, sending the most peculiar signals to her core. The wetness, so embarrassing already, pooled. Surely he would hear it, smell it. He would know.

Frances did not care. She wanted him. It no longer mattered that he did not love her, or even like her especially. She liked him well enough in this moment, and nothing else was of any consequence.

His tongue invaded and explored, twisting around hers to perform an erotic, sensual dance. He tickled that place behind her teeth, her lips, the roof of her mouth. It was all so… so knowing. And so intense.

Richard broke the kiss at last, and Frances might have stumbled had he not had his arms about her. He left her, quite literally, weak at the knees. She had heard such fanciful tales and had never believed them. She did now.

"I trust you can make our wedding arrangements speedily, Lady Frances, or we may find our marriage consummated prior to the event.

She could but nod, because the truth was, if he had tumbled her down into the hay and lifted her skirts, she would

97

not have said anything in protest. Blessed Virgin, she might even raise her skirts herself if she did not get out of there.

"I... I shall, yes. Of course." She took a step back. "Do you... do you always kiss women that way?"

His lips formed a smile which sent her senses reeling again. There was something lewd and suggestive in that amused expression, and a sincere promise of delights yet to be offered.

"Only those to whom I am betrothed," he replied.

"Betrothed? Well, yes, I suppose we are." Frances toyed with her new status in her head and decided she rather liked it. "I... I shall ask Mrs Lark to prepare a special meal this evening, to celebrate."

"Excellent plan. And I shall pen a letter to the king at once." He offered her his hand. "Will you walk back to the house with me?"

She shook her head. "I shall follow. I have another apple, for Athena. And I thought I might go for a ride since it is such a fine day."

"A fine day? Indeed it is. I shall find a groom to accompany you."

"That will not be necessary. I have always ridden alone."

He frowned and shook his head. "The fighting may be over, but the land is far from peaceful. There are too many dispossessed or defeated soldiers roaming the countryside, ready to rob the vulnerable. You will be accompanied if you mean to go beyond the walls of Castle Whitleigh, and the groom will be armed."

"Very well. If you insist." She trotted the few paces down the stable to where Athena waited patiently. The mare crunched on her apple while Frances beamed at her husband-to-be. "I shall send word to the kitchens while my horse is being saddled. And I shall see you at the evening meal, my lord."

Chapter Nine

The letter to His Majesty penned, Richard rolled the parchment into a scroll, sealed it, and tied it with a piece of red ribbon. He handed it to the messenger, who waited patiently at the door to the solar. "I shall see you to the drawbridge. And I wish you Godspeed and a safe journey back to London."

The man bowed and stowed the missive within his tunic. "My thanks for your hospitality, my lord."

Richard opened the door to the spiral stairs and gestured the man to precede him.

Out in the courtyard a horse was ready, saddled and waiting. With luck, his reply to the king would be in Henry's hands in the Tower of London by the day after tomorrow, or the day after that at most.

He shielded his eyes against the afternoon sun and watched as the man cantered over the drawbridge then set his mount to a gallop, heading for the Plymouth road. If Henry saw fit to reply at once, and there was no reason to suppose the king would delay, Richard anticipated the monarch's effusive congratulations and formal consent to the match would be with him within a sennight. Hopefully, he and Frances could marry soon after that, provided his bride was as good as her word and had made the necessary arrangements.

Not that much was required, not really. A priest must be sent for, he supposed, and there must be sufficient witnesses to ensure no dispute later. Doubtless the bride would require a fine new gown for the occasion. And, of course, there must be ample meat for the feasting, which he would see to. All quite simple.

He set off to return to the house but paused at the sound of approaching hoof beats.

Has the courier forgotten something? He swung around again, to be confronted not by the king's messenger, but by Athena, Frances' dainty little mare. The palfrey cantered across the drawbridge then slowed to a gentle trot. She pranced off in the direction of the stable.

The horse was riderless.

"Holy fuck," he breathed. "Where is Frances? And

99

what happened to her bloody escort?"

His second question was answered readily enough when the man he had instructed to ride with Frances scurried from the stables to catch the palfrey's trailing reins.

Richard strode forward. "What the fuck is going on here?" he demanded. "Did I not instruct you to accompany Lady Frances?"

The man, one of the soldiers under his command, bowed. "Aye, my lord. Ye did. An' I would have. I came here straight away, but 'er Ladyship were gone already."

"Gone?" He could scarcely believe it. "She left alone?"

The man shrugged. "I do not rightly know, my lord, as I did not see 'er leave."

"Who did, then? Someone must have saddled her palfrey and helped her to mount."

"Not necessarily, my lord." The elderly groom who had managed the stables prior to the fall of the house of de Whytte shuffled forward. "'Er Ladyship 'as been saddling 'er own mare for as long as I can recall. An' she would ha' used the mounting block over yonder."

Richard ground his teeth in impotent fury. Had he not specifically told the stubborn wench of the dangers of riding out alone? What if she had encountered thieves? Bandits? She might be dead in a ditch. Or worse.

"We must find her." His gaze fell upon Stephen, who had ventured out into the bailey to see what the commotion was about. "Frances is missing. Assemble a dozen men for a search party."

"Missing? How? Surely she had an escort."

"Do not even ask," Richard growled. He turned his icy glare on the hapless groom. "You. Saddle my stallion. I want him out here and ready to leave in two minutes."

The man hurried off to do the lord's bidding, Stephen at his heels.

Richard ran his hand through his hair and groaned. *Christ, what if we cannot find her? What if—?*

"My lord. I see her." The shout came from the

gatehouse, where the guardsman in charge of raising and lowering the drawbridge when required also acted as a lookout. "Is that not Lady Frances?"

Richard bounded over to the drawbridge and peered in the direction the man pointed. "Fuck, yes. It is." The small figure in the distance was on foot, and limping, but unmistakably it was Frances. "What the hell has happened to her?"

"My lord, your horse…" The groom led Trojan across the cobbles, ready and saddled, just as Richard had instructed.

Richard barely paused to thank the elderly servant before he leapt into the saddle and set off at a canter.

Frances was still at least a mile distant from the castle, but he reached her in only a couple of minutes. Her smile when she saw him approaching was bright enough to thaw an iceberg, but Richard was having none of that. He drew his mount to a halt and glared down at her.

"Richard. How kind of you to come out to meet me. I have twisted my ankle, I think. May I…" She reached up, clearly expecting him to swing her up before him on the mighty warhorse.

"What the fuck do you think you are doing?" he roared.

She stepped back, eyes widening. "I… I… Whatever do you mean?"

"I warned you not to ride alone."

"I know, but I was in a hurry. I was impatient to get back and speak to Mrs Lark, and my grandmother, so I thought perhaps he could catch me up."

"Oh? And you left word as to your direction, I suppose?"

"Well, no, but I always take the same route… She raised her hands again. "Please, Richard. My ankle throbs so…"

"The man I sent was one of my guards, not your servants. Did I not specifically say that your escort must be armed?"

"Well, yes, now that you mention it. But I simply assumed—"

101

He cut off her attempt to explain with a swipe of his hand. "What happened? Your mare arrived back without you."

"Athena is safe, then? Thank goodness."

"Aye. She is safe, which is more than you can claim for yourself, madam."

"I took a tumble, that is all. It has been a while since I have jumped the hedgerow at the top of the long meadow, and I must have misjudged it. I ended up in the ditch, and the last I saw of Athena she was heading for home."

"The damned mare has better sense than her mistress. I should make you hobble the rest of the way."

"Richard, please… It hurts, and—"

"Any discomfort in your ankle will be as nothing compared to that which I mean to inflict upon your bottom, madam. I trust you have heeded my words and have plenty of prepared switches readily to hand."

"Switches? You cannot mean to…" She clutched at his booted foot. "Not today. It is the day of our betrothal."

"Indeed so, and perfectly apt, therefore, that I should set out with no remaining room for doubt, exactly what will happen should you choose to disobey me. I consider obedience an essential quality in a wife, and it is timely that you should learn to adopt a suitably compliant attitude."

"I did not disobey. I intended to meet up with the man you sent, I have told you this."

He leaned down to offer her his hand. "Do not quibble with me on this matter. The moment you crossed the drawbridge unaccompanied, you disobeyed my express instructions and placed yourself in grave danger. I will not tolerate it. You are fortunate that your misadventure was not of a more serious nature."

She allowed him to haul her up onto the horse, then turned to smile at him. "It is kind of you to be concerned, but really, it is not necessary. I know this landscape as well as I know the back of my own hand, and I am personally acquainted with everyone who lives within twenty miles of Whitleigh."

Richard hauled in a frustrated sigh. "Did I not tell

you," he ground out the words, "there are desperate strangers roaming the land. No woman is safe alone." He grimaced when he considered the many and various dangers she had exposed herself to. "God's teeth, girl, can you even start to imagine what I feared when I saw that mare cantering back alone, the reins trailing in the dirt? I imagined you dead. Or raped. At best, lying unconscious in the mud."

"Oh. I did not realise. I… I am sorry to have worried you."

For the first time, he fancied he discerned a flash of contrition. "You will be, I have no doubt of that." He nudged Trojan into a steady canter and turned his head in the direction of home.

Back in the cobbled bailey, Richard slid from the saddle, then assisted Frances to dismount. She clung to him, holding her injured foot off the ground, while he passed the reins to the elderly groom with instructions to wipe the stallion down and see him safely back in his stall. Then, with no further ado or conversation, he swept Frances into his arms and strode up the front steps and into the hall.

Lady Margaret was seated by the roaring fire on the settle she favoured. The dowager got to her feet when she saw him approach, her granddaughter cradled in his arms.

"Is she all right? I heard that her mare returned alone…"

"Aye, she is well enough," Richard growled. "More by good fortune than by good sense, though." He set his burden down on the settle. "Frances has wrenched her ankle and finds it painful to put her weight on it."

"A cold compress, that is what is needed. I shall see to it."

"I shall leave you to dress the injury then and make her as comfortable as you can." He sent a stern glare Frances' way. "As for you, madam, you will present yourself in my solar in two hours. By that time my anger will have cooled sufficiently that I may deal properly with you."

"My lord, I—"

"Two hours, Frances. And you know what you must

103

bring with you. I believe we shall require at least a half dozen in order to adequately address the matter before us."

She was prompt, he would allow her that. Exactly two hours after he strode from the hall, Richard looked up from his rereading of the king's missive in response to the quiet tap on the door to the solar.

"Come in," he called.

She entered slowly, the limp still pronounced, though he noted that her right ankle was now swathed in a tight bandage.

"The compress did not entirely do the trick, then," he observed.

"It is better, I think." Despite her brave words, he noted that with her free hand she grasped the back of the chair closest to her and used it to support her weight. In her other hand she clutched a bundle of wet switches, still dripping from having recently been removed from the water used to keep them supple.

"Put them on the table," he commanded.

She did so, and he eyed them with interest. She had obeyed his instructions in this, at least. The switches were narrow, guaranteed to deliver an edifying sting, but each had been carefully trimmed with all sharp edges removed. He picked up the one closest to him and drew his fingertips along its length.

"You did well, Frances. I believe I will be able to make the coming minutes suitably memorable for you with these." He eyed her beneath his brows. "Given your existing injury, and the discomfort I mean to inflict very shortly, I will understand if you prefer to delay our betrothal celebrations for a day or two."

"You still mean to wed me, then?" She tipped up her chin in that challenging manner that had become familiar to him.

He regarded her more closely. She lowered her gaze, her underlying anxiety more apparent now. This was to be expected, though he had assumed her attitude to be associated

104

with the imminent prospect of a switching rather than her longer-term future.

"Of course. That is what this is about, to some extent. If our marriage is to be a success, that will depend upon you learning to respect my authority, as well as taking proper care over your own safety." He softened his gaze. "Having got this far, I do not wish to lose you, Frances."

"I... do you not?"

"Of course I do not. Your safety and well-being are important to me. I... care about you."

"I did not realise. I thought... I mean, you only..." She paused, drew in a breath, then, "I had thought ours to be a marriage of convenience, intended to appease the king."

"On your side, perhaps. Not on mine. I am faced with no requirement to appease our monarch. I do not need to wed. Henry will not press me on the matter. But I chose to take a bride. And I chose you."

Her mouth formed a perfect little 'O'.

"So, you will appreciate that I have no desire to attend your funeral before we have the opportunity to celebrate our wedding."

"My... funeral?"

"Aye. It is not my wish to curtail your freedoms, but I mean to ensure your safety to the best of my ability. For this, I must have your absolute obedience. These fine switches you have prepared will assist me in that endeavour. And be under no illusion, Frances, I will not hesitate to repeat this lesson as often as necessary. It has become clear to me that you possess a wilful streak which I find disturbing. I mean to curtail your recklessness, whatever it takes."

"I... I am neither wilful nor reckless." She tipped up her chin again and stiffened her spine. "I made a mistake, that is all. A misunderstanding."

He gave a wry chuckle. "Another 'misunderstanding'. Was some part of 'you must be escorted when out riding' in any way unclear?"

"Well, no, but—"

"I can see we are getting nowhere, so this discussion is over. I will make my point in a more direct manner. You will undress, if you please, and lean over the table."

"Richard. My lord, please…"

"Now, Frances." He hardened his tone. With the possible exception of Stephen, it was a tone which produced instant obedience from his men. This diminutive female should be no match at all.

And so it appeared to be. Her complexion distinctly pale, she started to unfasten her wool gown. It was a simple enough garment, not requiring assistance, and within a couple of short minutes she stood naked before him. If her nudity embarrassed her, she concealed the fact well, making no attempt to cover herself. The bandage on her ankle seemed oddly incongruous, but of course, he would not require her to remove that.

"Loosen your hair, too."

"My hair?" She reached for the braid. "But why…?"

He could not rightly say, save that it was a look he preferred. He settled for a simple, "Do as I say, Frances."

She unwound the narrow ribbon which secured the plait then shook her hair free. It fell in lush waves to her hips, the colour of sunlight and ripening corn. He resisted the urge to take a hank of it in his fist. *Perhaps later…*

"I would normally require your feet to be on the floor, but in view of your indisposition, I shall make an exception on this occasion. You may kneel on a chair, then lean forward and rest your upper body on the tabletop." He dragged a chair into position, turning it so the back was at right angles to the table. He would not permit this improvised arrangement to impede his strokes at all. "Get yourself ready, Frances. Remember, your bottom must be held up nice and high, in readiness to receive the full impact of these excellent switches of yours."

He believed he might have heard a muffled sob as she eased herself up onto the chair. Then, slowly, she lowered her shoulders until her upper body and cheek rested against the polished oak.

"Your bottom needs to be higher, Frances," he observed, whilst treating himself to an excellent view of her perfect posterior. The pale globes of her buttocks presented a

106

most fetching sight, one which would be substantially enhanced by the well-earned stripes he meant to paint on the milky canvass she presented.

Frances obligingly shuffled closer to the edge of the table, elevating her heart-shaped bottom the requisite few inches.

"That will be just fine. Now, you will remain in that position until I tell you that we are finished. Please repeat that back to me in order that I am quite sure you have understood."

"I... I will remain still. Until you tell me we are finished."

She was already close to tears. Best to press on and get this unpleasantness over with. "Do you have any questions, Frances? Any uncertainty regarding the reasons for this punishment?"

She shook her head. "I should not have left the castle without my escort."

Ah. At last. It never ceased to amaze Richard how clear-headed a woman could become, once she was naked and up-ended for a spanking.

"The switches are by your right hand. You will select one and pass it to me, please." He had also observed that added effect might be achieved by requiring a woman to participate in her own chastisement.

Frances' hand shook when she passed him the first switch. He accepted it, then took a moment to consider his options.

"I do believe that we will require more than just one, to properly attract and hold your attention. Pass me another, please."

"Sir?" she whimpered. "You mean... to use two. At the same time?"

"Exactly." He stroked her quivering bottom with the switch he already held. "Quickly, please. I am sure we both have other things to do this day. The sooner this business is concluded, the sooner we can get on."

"Two will be too much. Please, my lord..."

"I disagree. Two will be perfect. If I am obliged to reach for the switch myself, I shall not be best pleased."

She groaned and stretched out her arm to select a second twig.

Suitably equipped, Richard settled the pair of switches in his palm and shook them. Droplets of water spattered Frances' upturned bottom. He tried a couple of experimental sweeps through the air, satisfied at the high-pitched whistle he created.

"Are you ready, Frances?"

"No," she wailed.

"I see. Then we shall wait here, just as we are, until you tell me to proceed. There is no hurry."

"I thought you said we both had better things to do."

"Ah, but you are my priority, Frances. You have my undivided attention for as long as it is required, so do, please, take your time."

"I hate you," she muttered. "You are cruel, and… and…"

"I do not believe you hate me, or at least, not entirely." He swiped his free hand between her legs to stroke her soft folds and brought his palm away wet. "Your body does not hate me, nor does it object greatly to what is happening. Your arousal, curious though it may seem, is clear and undeniable."

"I am not aroused. I just…"

"Yes, you are. Though I do not deny that you are very afraid, also. The two are not incompatible." He continued to stroke her cunny as he spoke, smearing her wetness over her delicate inner thighs." If you take your punishment well, and I find myself satisfied as to your genuine contrition, I would not be averse to pleasuring you after, should you so desire."

"You… you should not touch me there," she protested, though unless he was sorely mistaken, she also parted her thighs, just a fraction.

"We are to be wed. I shall touch you as I please." He proved his point by sliding one long finger into her slick channel. "Do you like this, Frances?"

"It is wrong. You should not—"

"I asked if you like it, not for a lecture on morality.

So, do you like me to touch you in this manner?" He drove his finger in and out, then added a second.

Her channel tightened around his fingers. Frances moaned, the vocalisation mixing prettily with the sounds of her increased wetness.

"Answer me, Frances," he urged.

"I… I cannot…"

"Then allow me to explain your current predicament. I can continue with this little game, and by the sound of your pants and moans, and the way your cunny quivers around my fingers, I fully anticipate that quite soon you will arrive at your climax. However, I would be obliged to take a dim view of that, since it is entirely inappropriate for you to receive pleasure before you have properly atoned for your wrongdoing. Should you be so careless, you will incur further punishment, and I do not believe you want that. All you need do, to stop me, is answer my question. And, you will answer truthfully." He paused for a moment. "So, do you like me to touch you in this manner? Does it give you pleasure, Frances?"

"Yes," she ground out. "It does."

"Thank you." He drew his fingers from her body. "Now, all that is required in order for us to proceed, is your agreement that you are quite ready to receive your switching."

She heaved in a deep breath, then, "I am ready. Please, just do what you must."

Chapter Ten

White-hot pain exploded. Agony snaked across her upturned buttocks, cruel, exquisitely ferocious. Merciless.

Frances let out a shriek, her fists clenched. She fought to suck in the next precious breath.

The air whistled once more. Fire crackled across her skin. Again, she screamed, unable to contain her cries.

When the third stroke landed, she truly believed she could bear no more and sagged against the table in abject defeat.

"Lift up your bottom," came the intractable command. "We are not done yet."

"I… I cannot. It is too much…"

"Up," he instructed, tapping her inflamed buttocks with the tips of the switches.

Faced with no other choice, Frances heaved herself back into position. She was sobbing, unable to contain the outpouring of her response. If she had found his belt daunting, that was as nothing compared to this.

He swung again. The switches connected at a spot just above the previous stroke. Frances' breath left her lungs in a sharp gasp, and she braced for the next.

It did not come. Instead, Richard dropped the switches on the table to her left. "Those are worn now. I shall trouble you for two more, please."

"Wh-what?"

"Two more switches, please. Be quick."

She extended her hand, blindly seeking the remaining pile. She passed him two fresh twigs.

"Thank you. I believe we shall wear these out, and the remaining two. Then, we shall have a discussion, you and I, following which I shall decide whether to send for more switches or consider our problem resolved."

Frances gritted her teeth. It would be resolved, she promised herself that much. There would be no call for more switches.

The next few strokes fell hard and unrelenting. Her

bottom was aflame, she could not doubt it. Without thinking, she found herself reaching back, not to protect herself but to check for the presence of blood. Richard paused.

"Shall I tie your hands, Frances?"

"I am sorry," she wailed. "I wanted to know if I was bleeding."

"Of course you are not. I will not do you lasting harm. I have told you this."

Had he? She could not recall. She found it hard to think straight, to remember anything beyond the fact that she hurt. Her world was one great knot of pain, and she knew nothing beyond that.

"Please, how much more. I… I cannot bear it."

"I will not ask you to endure more than you are able, but I will make the point that is needed. You must learn obedience, and you must learn it now."

"I have, I swear. I shall never disobey you again."

Richard chuckled. "It does not surprise me to hear you say that." He laid his palm on her smarting bottom and massaged gently. "A woman will usually swear to anything by this stage."

"I am telling the truth," she protested. "I… I know I should not have gone out alone…"

"No, you should not have done so, since it has brought you to this. But, will you remember your promise the next time you are tempted to think you know better and can disregard my instructions?"

"I will remember. I swear that I will."

"Perhaps, though I mean to be sure on that point before we will be done here. I believe we can get another stroke or two out of this pair, then we shall wear out the other two. 'Tis a pity, I suppose, from your point of view, that your bottom is so tender, since the switches seem to be holding up very well."

Frances groaned and clenched the tender bottom in question, an instant before the next stroke descended to set her flesh alight once more.

As good as his word, Richard got another exquisitely agonising stroke out of the switches before he considered them past their usefulness. He discarded them with the first pair.

"Pass me the remaining ones, please."

There was no point in protesting, in pleading, begging, promising, or weeping for mercy. Frances groped for the switches, found them, and handed them to Richard. He thanked her, then took up his position behind her again.

"I know that you are sorry. I believe you when you tell me that you are determined to do better in the future. These final strokes will serve to cement that resolve, and I hope you will accept them in that spirit."

She did not answer, could find nothing to say. Frances tensed, ready to endure these final few strokes and hoping that she would do so with at least a semblance of fortitude.

He raised his arm. She clenched her buttocks, only to let out an agonised howl when the onslaught shifted to the backs of her thighs.

"Ah, I believe I have your full attention now." He raised his arm again and delivered the next two strokes in rapid succession.

Frances could barely catch her breath. She had deluded herself into thinking that she had discovered a level of coping where she might endure what was happening, but now found herself engulfed in searing agony beyond anything which had gone before. She writhed against the table, unable to remain still however much he might demand it of her. She no longer sobbed or cried out. Her throat was raw, and she could only emit inarticulate grunts as the following two strokes rained down on her delicate flesh.

"Hmm, I think we must stop now."

She twisted her neck to observe him through her tears. Richard examined the switches with care, then met her gaze. "Somewhat frayed, I fear. Shall we set these aside and have our discussion now?"

She closed her eyes but managed a nod.

"I would invite you to sit upright, or even stand, but I do not believe you would find relief either way. Allow me to assist you." He gently raised her so she knelt upright, then slid his arms around her and lifted her from the chair.

Still naked, it never occurred to Frances to suggest that she might get dressed again. Instead, she clung to his tunic when he sat down on the chair and arranged her on his lap, her punished bottom suspended between his spread thighs and her injured ankle off the floor.

"I do not suppose you to be especially comfortable," he observed in a dry tone, "but this will have to suffice. So now, you may explain to me what obedience actually means, and how you intend to satisfy my requirements in the future."

"I… I…"

"I am waiting, Frances."

"I do not know," she managed at last. "I want to be a good wife. I want to… to… be happy, with you. I want you to be happy, and proud of me."

"I *am* proud of you," he stated. "I have already said that I admire your courage and loyalty. And now, I have seen that you can accept punishment as an adult woman should."

"I want to be a good wife to you," she repeated. "I… I always imagined I would marry and have children. That my husband would love me, and I would love him." She managed to get the words out, despite her sobs.

"Then, let us strive for that, Frances."

"But do you forgive me?" She sobbed harder. "Do you trust me? You cannot love me if you do not have faith in me."

"Faith, and trust, will come. They must be earned. And I must earn yours every bit as much as you need to earn mine. We will have time to work on that in the years to come. But know this, Frances de Whytte, and know it now. I care about you, and when I thought you might be hurt, or lost to me forever, I cannot begin to describe the horror I felt in those moments. I never wish to experience such fear again."

Frances could not conceal her astonishment. "Fear? You? But you are fearless. A warrior."

"Fear takes many forms, Frances, as does love." He kissed the top of her head. "Earlier, you said that you hate me."

"I said that before, the first time you spanked me..

113

It… It was not true then, and it is not true now. I apologise. I will not say it again."

He chuckled. "For the most part, I shall punish you for what you do, not what you say. Especially if we are alone. I would have your honesty, always, so you will speak freely to me."

"It was not a kind thing to say, even so."

"In the circumstances, a degree of… ambivalence… was to be expected. But while we are on this delicate subject, may I enquire as to the current level of your arousal?"

"My…?"

He bent lower to murmur in her ear, "Are you still wet, Frances? And more to the point, do you wish me to do anything about it?"

"That is a wicked suggestion, sir." *But still…*

"But you are tempted anyway," he insisted.

"I am not. I just… oh!"

She trembled on his lap when he swiped his palm through her dripping folds again.

"Spread your legs, Frances," he urged.

"I should not…"

"But you will. Do it, my sweet slut. Spread for me."

She should have been insulted by what he had called her, but she was not. Perversely, Frances decided that she wanted to be his slut. His alone. Slowly, she parted her thighs.

"Lie back against me, sweetheart, Relax. Allow me to pleasure you."

Yes. Yes…

His touch was clever. Expert. He stroked her, traced the outline of her entrance, then thrust his fingers within. Her body parted willingly to accept the intrusion, to welcome him.

He found that special place, that sweet spot where his caresses felt even more intense, even more… everything.

"Richard," she groaned. "I want…"

"I know. You shall have what you want because you have earned it, by accepting your punishment and acknowledging what you did wrong." He inserted another finger, stretching her beautifully, and twisted his hand to somehow increase the delectable friction.

"What are you doing?" she moaned. "It feels so… so wonderful. I think I… I want…"

Frances was utterly confused. She should resent his touch, want nothing other than to be out of his company, left alone to nurse her humiliation and lick her wounds. She felt nothing of the sort. Instead, it was as though a glorious prize dangled, somewhere just beyond her reach. If she could only stretch out, if she could grasp it, hold it, and… and…

"Oh! Ooooh." Something shattered deep at her core. The pleasure was exquisite, sweeping aside any residual discomfort. She writhed in his lap, helpless in her desire, soaking up every last tremor and shudder of her release.

He must know what was happening to her — how could he not? Richard drew out the final ripples of pleasure, his skilled touch continuing to soothe and calm her as the storm of emotion abated. Only when she finally lay still in his arms did he slide his fingers from her near-boneless body.

"Are you cold?" he asked her softly. "You are shivering."

She shook her head. "I do not think so."

"I should have punished you in your chamber, or mine. Then, after, I could have tucked you up in bed."

"I do not wish to go to bed, my lord."

"Oh? What, then?"

Her stomach emitted a low growl. "I believe I would like to enjoy my betrothal feast. Do you suppose it is too late now to ask Mrs Lark to prepare something suited to the occasion?"

"You sent word to her before your reckless adventure, did you not?"

"Well, yes, but…"

"Then, from what I have seen of Mrs Lark, we should have no fear that she will be other than equal to the task. I expect a fine banquet awaits."

"I should get dressed." At last, good sense prevailed.

The earl seemed to concur. "Indeed. That would be preferable if you mean to appear in the hall this evening. Are you sure you feel up to it?"

She nodded. "I am famished. Perhaps I might contrive to use a cushion to soften my seat. Do you think anyone will notice? And there is always my grandmother's salve…" Cautiously, she set her good foot on the floor. "I wonder, would you assist me with my clothes?"

Frances returned to her chamber to apply a generous coating of salve to her punished bottom. She exclaimed in stunned surprise at the state of her flesh when she twisted to examine her buttocks in the looking glass. As promised, her skin was intact. She was stunned to see that Richard could inflict such pain yet leave her relatively undamaged, and for the first time she pondered the distinct possibility that he must have had practice.

A lot of practice.

A pang of something she recognised as jealousy clouded her thoughts, just for a moment. She dismissed it ruthlessly. Richard was to wed her, not any other woman from his past. None of what may have gone before was of any consequence now.

She applied the salve, then rearranged her clothing. She even managed to rebraid her hair, though it was not so easy since she was unable to sit before her looking glass. By the time she was ready to go down, her stomach growled impatiently. She had not eaten since early that morning. Halfway down the main stairs she was greeted by the tantalising aromas wafting up, testimony to Mrs Lark's culinary arts.

Cheers greeted her when she stepped into the great hall. News of the betrothal had circulated quickly. Her people and those who had arrived with Richard were all assembled, and all appeared equally delighted to celebrate the joining of the two houses. Tankards were banged on the trestle tables running the length of the hall, and all rose to greet her.

Frances paused, momentarily overwhelmed. She had expected an appetising meal and a degree of merrymaking, but not this.

116

Richard stepped down from the top table to arrive at her side. He kissed her, first on the forehead, then on the mouth, before offering her his elbow.

Frances was glad of his aid in taking her seat, since her ankle was almost as tender as her backside.

"I have had a cushion placed on your chair," he murmured.

"Thank you," she replied, tucking her hand in the crook of his arm. "The food smells wonderful."

She settled herself into her seat at Richard's right hand, taking particular care when she finally placed her weight on her bottom. She stifled a groan and instead concentrated on the array of food.

Bowls of thick, steaming pottage were set at intervals along the table. Frances knew full well how deliciously satisfying Mrs Lark's hearty soup would be and requested a bowl to start her meal.

Mrs Lark did not disappoint. The pottage was every bit as tasty and hearty as she expected, made with fresh vegetables and, she believed, some meat, too. Rabbit, probably. She must ask. Later.

The second course consisted of a generous array of meats and fish. She and Richard shared a trencher which he heaped with venison and wild boar, the spoils of his most recent hunting expedition, as well as salmon and pike from the River Tavy. Frances used her small eating dagger to spear the pieces of meat and lift them to her mouth. There was wine, too, and mead, as well as the copious quantities of ale required to properly celebrate such an occasion.

By the time she reached the main course, an elaborate confection of roast swan flavoured with herbs and garnished with slivers of baked fruits, Frances was convinced she could eat not another mouthful. She was wrong. The roast was even more delicious that the previous courses, and it did not take much urging on Richard's part to convince her to fill the trencher again.

It was much later in the evening, though, before she could be persuaded to enjoy a little of the dessert. Mrs Lark had prepared a selection of tiny sweet tarts and pastries,

117

crushed nuts doused in honey, and autumn berries soaked in syrup. By the time they arrived at the final course of candied fruit and nibbles of cheese, Frances truly believed she would not require food again for at least a month.

"No more, really." She shook her head when a serving lad offered her a dish of candied pears. "I believe I would burst if I took one more mouthful."

Richard, too, settled back in his chair and waved away any more delicacies. He offered her that lop sided smile. "I trust the feast met your expectations."

She nodded, then, "Will ours be a long betrothal?"

"I sincerely hope not. I have sent word to Henry and expect to hear his reply quickly. I suggest we make the arrangements for one week from today."

"One week?" Frances gaped at him. "Did you say one week?"

"Aye."

"But…" Frances' mind was reeling. How could she possibly make the necessary preparations in just seven days? She must send for a priest, and there would need to be flowers. More feasting, of course. And a gown… what would she wear? "We will need more time than that. There is so much to be done…"

"A week," he insisted. "Provided we have the king's permission by then, I do not intend to delay any longer." He turned to where Lady Margaret sat on his other side. "No doubt we may rely upon your assistance, my lady."

"Naturally." The dowager nibbled on a piece of pear. "I have already taken the liberty of sending word to the holy fathers at Falstone priory in the hope that they will be able to provide someone to officiate, though of course that is not really necessary. A simple exchange of vows before witnesses would suffice."

"Quite," Richard agreed. "The ceremony will take place at the doors to the chapel here at Whitleigh."

"Even so," Frances tried again, "we shall need to prepare another feast. Mrs Lark will need time to plan."

"You underestimate our cook, Frances. Not to

mention the state of our larders." The dowager reached to pat her hand. "Allow me and Mrs Lark to worry about those details. You should concentrate on ensuring you have a gown worthy of the occasion."

"Well, there is that. I have no fabric suitable for a wedding gown. I would need to send to Plymouth, or… or…"

"What about that bolt of duck-egg blue silk which you have been saving for just the right occasion. Is this not such an event?"

"Well, yes…" Frances had purchased the material over a year previously, from a traveling merchant. It had been a ridiculous extravagance, but her brother had insisted and handed over the purse of coins.

"So, that is decided. Sara has a deft touch with a needle, and she will be able to help you make the gown. Leave the rest to me."

"But I could not possibly trouble you so."

"Nonsense. I shall enjoy myself. Permit an old lady some indulgences, if you please."

"Grandmêre, I cannot—"

"Enough. All is in hand." Richard rose to his feet and offered her his hand. "Provided we have the king's consent by then, we shall be wed one week from today. So, now that the details are settled, let us all raise a glass to the future."

The people of Castle Whitleigh required no further urging. Glasses were held aloft, and cheers rang out calling for the health, happiness, and prosperity of the duke and his bride-to-be.

Frances fell silent. The matter was settled. In a week's time, she would become the next Duchess of Whitleigh.

Chapter Eleven

"So, you mean to go through with this, then." It was a statement, not a question.

Richard regarded his brother through narrowed eyes and quirked his lip. "I do. Did you imagine otherwise?"

Stephen offered him a wry smile. "A man is entitled to hope. There is still time to stand aside and permit me to take your place. I would be prepared to make the sacrifice…"

"That will not be necessary," Richard muttered. "Now, cease your babbling. My bride is here."

"Ah, well, if you cannot be dissuaded from this reckless course, I suppose I must accept defeat with good grace. You are a fortunate man, brother. She is delightful."

Richard had already arrived at that conclusion. He patted his brother's shoulder in mock commiseration. "She is. And in the absence of such a prize for yourself, you must be content with your new title and lands."

Stephen grinned. "Who says I am not in possession of a similar prize? I was merely offering to assist my brother in his hour of need, as any decent man should."

"The delightful Sara has forgiven you, then?"

Stephen shrugged. "She is warming to me, I believe." His expression grew more serious. "So, Henry has agreed to your other request also?"

"He has. You are now the Earl of Romsey. My congratulations on your elevation, brother."

"You would truly relinquish your old title so readily?"

Richard replied without hesitation. His decision had been made some time ago, and it only remained to carry it out. He was well satisfied with his part of the bargain. "I have said so, have I not? My place is here now. I am not prepared to scurry back and forth like an eager puppy, so Keeterly needs a new master, one able to devote himself to managing the keep, and I can think of none better suited. Or more deserving. Clearly, Henry thinks so, too. What you were denied by an accident of birth is now yours by merit, in recognition of your service to our king." He slapped his brother on the back, then stepped forward to greet his bride.

The gown she had fashioned in such haste was exquisite, though if he was being perfectly honest, Richard preferred his bride wearing rather less. Even so, he could not fault the vision of loveliness she presented as she moved to take the place occupied until a few moments ago by his brother. Frances positioned herself beside him at the door to the chapel and peered up at him nervously. Richard winked. She flushed and directed her gaze downwards.

The priest from Falstone Priory had arrived two days previously, just hours before the messenger from the king. As well as consenting to Stephen's new station in life, Henry expressed himself delighted with the turn of events regarding Richard's marriage plans and offered his heartiest felicitations. What was more, he professed himself eager to make the acquaintance of the new duchess when the pair attended his own wedding in a mere six weeks' time.

Richard had yet to inform Frances that her presence was expected at court. She would require some convincing, but ultimately, she would do what must be done. His new bride appreciated better than most the importance of appeasing their monarch.

Frances' small hand rested in his much larger one. Her fingers felt cold. He squeezed them, then glanced down to offer her a reassuring smile.

Her face was pale. And he had noted the remains of a slight limp when she had made her way down the gravelled pathway leading to the chapel to take her place beside him. He had insisted that she rest her injured ankle, and as far as he was aware she had done so. He had hardly seen her at all over the previous week, and when he enquired as to her whereabouts had been assured she was keeping to her chamber, busily engaged in dress fittings and preparing the flowers which now adorned the chapel entrance. He supposed her gait would have been far more laboured had she not obeyed him, and it was obvious from the perfection he now admired that she had taken her duties seriously.

The blue silk draped seductively about her breasts and

hips, and a length had been set aside to create a soft veil to cover her pale curls. Her sole item of jewellery was a simple blue gemstone, a sapphire, he fancied, on a length of silver chain. Richard believed he had seen the bauble before, worn by Lady Margaret.

He vaguely recalled hearing that Edmund De Whytte had taken the family treasures with him when he had fled, so Richard supposed Frances was not now spoilt for choice. He would start to rectify that, beginning with the pearl earrings he had acquired for her as a wedding gift.

He slipped the trinkets from his pocket and reached for her chin. He tipped her face up, winked at her again, then showed her the pearls nestling on his palm.

"For me?" she whispered.

He inclined his head, then swept the edge of her veil aside with the backs of his knuckles to expose her small earlobe. He pinned one earring in place, then the other.

"I… I have no gift for you," she murmured. "I never thought…"

He leaned in, his words for her alone. "You do have a gift for me, and I shall enjoy savouring it later."

"Richard!" She flushed an even deeper shade of pink, and his cock twitched.

Fuck, this is going to be a good day. And an even better night.

He schooled his thoughts and unruly cock into a semblance of respectability and directed his attention to the matter at hand. Behind them, their entire household had gathered. Stephen took his place beside Lady Margaret, arms folded, his features set in a serious line as he observed the proceedings about to unfold. He and Lady Margaret would be the official witnesses, but all would observe the exchange of vows. The older lady smiled softly, her lined face perhaps the most serene of all those present.

The priest cleared his throat. The bride and groom turned to face him.

"Are we ready to begin, my lord?" The holy father seemed as eager to get on with the business as Richard's cock was.

"Please, commence."

The next few minutes passed quickly. Vows were exchanged, his own voice loud and clear, that of his bride more muted. Richard observed her throughout. She appeared nervous, and he supposed that was to be expected, but not unduly reluctant or hesitant. Her fingers shook only very slightly when she extended her hand to receive his ring, the same bright-gold band with which his parents had been wed, sent hurriedly from Keeterly Castle in accordance with his hastily penned instructions. It looked well on her slender finger, in Richard's considered opinion.

The vows completed, the newly married couple accompanied the priest into the chapel, followed by their entourage who crowded in behind them to bear witness to the mass about to be celebrated in order to ensure the Lord's blessing upon the new union.

The priest took his duties seriously, Richard acknowledged, perhaps a little too much so. His own tolerance for draughty chapels and religious devotions was never especially pronounced and had more or less reached the limit of his endurance by the time the zealous clergyman responded to Richard's pointed throat-clearing. He ceased his fervent beseeching of the Good Lord and instead called the proceedings to a close, declaring the duke and duchess married in the sight of God and man.

Richard offered up his own heartfelt thanks, kissed Frances soundly on the mouth, then offered his arm to his duchess to lead her from the chapel. Their wedding feast awaited, and more besides.

In the main hall, Mrs Lark had surpassed even her exacting standards. The tables groaned under the weight of roast meats, delicately poached fish, seasonal vegetables, hearty pottage, and succulent fruits. Richard led Frances up onto the raised dais, then handed her into her seat. He remained standing until all were assembled. He waited patiently as Lady Margaret, splendid in her finest burgundy taffeta, was assisted up the few steps by Stephen. She beamed her approval at Richard before taking her seat next to Frances.

Only when all were present did he raise his tankard.

"To my beautiful duchess," he announced, "and to a glorious future for Castle Whitleigh and all who dwell here. And to our most gracious sovereign, King Henry the Seventh. God save and protect His Majesty." He took a generous swill of ale.

"The duchess, the duchess," came back the answering roar of approval. The shouts for the king were perhaps less enthusiastic in some quarters but sufficient to convince Richard that his strategy for uniting his fractured household and estates showed promise.

Richard settled in his seat, reached for Frances' hand, then gestured to the servants. Let the feasting begin.

It was still early, not yet past the hour of four o'clock in the afternoon, but Richard was determined to wait no longer before claiming what was now his to take. He murmured his desire in her ear as they toyed with the final round of sweetmeats, suggesting that they retire to the duke's chamber rather than linger in the hall.

Frances agreed readily enough, though he was aware of her discomfort at being escorted up the stairs and into the bedchamber by her grandmother, Stephen, and several more of her new husband's more senior military commanders.

The act of first bedding was not considered a private affair for couples such as they. Quite the reverse. The family and friends of the newly married couple would want to endorse the union and the king would require a detailed report of the proceedings. Such an account must include clear testimony that the marriage had been duly executed, witnessed and consummated, and therefore rendered unbreakable.

For his own part, Richard did not much care whether the audience stayed or left, but it was obvious that his new bride would find the entire affair deeply upsetting were she to lose her virginity before half a dozen witnesses. He only permitted their entourage to remain long enough to see the pair of them safely installed in the bedchamber together before ordering them all to leave them to it.

124

Stephen was the last to leave., He took Frances' cool hand and kissed her fingers, then winked at his brother. "Should you require any assistance, anything at all, do please feel free to summon me."

Richard's response was succinct

"Fuck off."

As soon as the door closed on Stephen's retreating back Richard crossed the room to lock it. They were alone at last.

"Are you afraid?" Richard leaned against the door and regarded his bride in the fading sunlight.

Frances stood in the centre of the bedchamber, her chin held aloft. Despite a tendency to lace and unlace her fingers, a sure indicator of her trepidation, she met his gaze with confidence. "No, I am not afraid."

"Good." He advanced to take her face between his palms. "You should not fear me, not here, in our chamber. Not in this matter."

"I… I do not fear you in any matter, my lord."

Now he lifted one eyebrow. He knew that assertion not to be entirely true, or, if it was, that failing on her part would be easily rectified. But not now. Such a discussion was for another time.

"Should I… should I remove my gown?" she asked.

Richard considered that to be an excellent suggestion. "Do you require help?"

"Perhaps if you could summon Sara…"

"That seems a pity, having just got rid of everyone. Allow me," he insisted, twirling a finger to indicate that she should present her back to him.

"Are you certain you know how…?"

"Believe me, I shall be equal to the task," he assured her, already freeing the ties which held her bodice in place. "This is a beautiful gown, by the way. You did well."

"Thank you, but I cannot take the credit. Sara worked so hard to make sure it was finished in time." She raised her hands to clasp the silk to her bosom as it slackened and would have fallen away.

"Then we shall take the utmost care not to damage it,

shall we?" Richard loosened the fastenings at the waist and knelt to peel the swathes of pale blue down to her ankles. "Perhaps if you could step out…"

Frances placed a hand on his shoulder for balance and did as he asked. She now stood before him in just her pretty cotton shift and delicate blue slippers. The light from the late afternoon sun shining through the unshuttered window created a most enticing silhouette.

Richard's cock twitched and swelled, not to be denied a second time. Still, he remained on his knees and lifted each foot in turn to remove the elegant shoes and set those aside with the gown. He stood again, rearranged his fast-hardening cock within his breeches, and set the discarded items of clothing, neatly folded, on a chest. Frances' gaze never left him as he moved about the chamber, and he knew she could not fail to note the bulge in his clothing.

"You are… you are very…. Oh," she offered.

He leaned against the chest, arms folded, and admired the fetching outline of her slender body beneath the near-translucent garment which hung to her knees. Richard contemplated ordering her to remove that, also, but decided it made near enough no difference. In any case, he found the eroticism of her almost nakedness beguiling. The dark triangle marking the junction of her thighs was clear to see, as were the pair of sharp points created by her swollen, erect nipples. He had ordered the fire lit much earlier so the room was pleasantly warm, leaving but one explanation.

"Your arousal intrigues me, Lady Frances. It is most becoming in my duchess, I think."

"Y-your duchess…?"

"Mine." He closed the distance between then, took her face between his hands, and kissed her.

Frances' lips parted for him, and he swept his tongue into her warmth. He released her face, only to tunnel his fingers into her hair, freeing the intricate braid. He swiftly shook the tresses free, enjoying the way they tumbled down her back as far as her hips. Richard broke the kiss long enough to bury his nose in her hair, inhaling the subtle tones of rosewater and lavender, tinged with something rather more earthy.

The musk of her growing response taunted his cock. His erection hardened, demanding release.

Not yet. We have more pressing business.

Richard groaned and swept Frances into his arms, then deposited her in the centre of his huge bed. She looked up at him, her expression a mix of surprise, anticipation, and apprehension. Her eyes deepened to a brilliant shade of cobalt. She ran hr tongue over her lower lip, then caught the same lip between her teeth.

Words of reassurance would only go so far, Richard decided. The time had come to show her, not tell her, that there was pleasure to be had here in his bed.

Leaning on one elbow, he lowered his face to hers once more, but this time the kiss was brief. He left a trail of light kisses across her shoulder, then worked his way down between her full breasts until the neckline of the shift prevented further progress.

"Shall I take it off?" she whispered helpfully.

He shook his head. "Not yet." Richard shifted his position, meaning to start his journey again, but this time at her feet. He lifted her right foot and kissed the instep, then did the same with the left.

Frances watched, her brow furrowing slightly. It was plain that she did not comprehend what he might be about. No matter. All would be clear soon enough.

He worked his way from her ankle to her knee, nuzzling, licking, kissing.

Frances jerked her leg. "That tickles."

He grinned at her. "Then you will need to strive to remain still for me, my lady."

She frowned, then gasped when he shoved the hem of her shift up to her mid thighs.

Gently, firmly, he eased her legs apart, then continued with his work. He traced a soft trail of kisses from her knees and up her inner thighs, halting when he almost reached that alluring dark triangle still visible beneath the thin fabric. As he worked his way higher, so he eased her thighs farther apart.

127

"My lord, what are you doing?" she demanded when he finally planted a kiss right on her mound, only the sheer barrier of her shift preventing him from nuzzling those curls also.

He looked up at her, met her wide-eyed blue gaze with his own. "Reach up and take hold of the headboard," he ordered her. "Do not let go and do not move."

"My lord?"

"Do as I say, Frances." His tone was low, not rough, but he would have his way. Here, in his bed, Richard would be absolute master.

Perhaps something in the timbre of his words conveyed that message to his perplexed little bride. Certainly, she was quick enough to obey. Once he was satisfied she understood her role in this endeavour, he returned to his task.

Now, he did peel back the shift as far as her waist. He buried his nose in the nest of honey-blonde curls and filled his nostrils with the delicate musk. Christ's bones, but she was lovely. True perfection.

He placed his hands on the inside of each knee and pressed outwards. He was gentle but firm. She did not resist, allowing him to spread her out, to admire her at his leisure.

Her inner folds, already swollen and darkening to a deep and rosy pink, glistened as moisture pooled. Richard took a moment to savour what was now his.

God's Balls, and I have not even touched her yet...

He slid his hands up her thighs until they rested a mere fraction away from her core.

Frances' breath hitched, but still she remained motionless.

He used his thumbs to part the lips of her entrance, then, before she could react, he lowered his head and drew the flat of his tongue along the entire length of her sex.

Frances let out a startled squeal and jerked violently.

"Be still," he growled.

"But... But you—"

"Do not move," he repeated, then licked her again.

"Richard, you cannot..."

128

He ignored her protests and continued to tease her plump folds, drawing the tip of his tongue around the quivering lips and then spearing inside.

"Oh, sweet Virgin…"

He was spurred on by Frances' breathless moans. It was obvious that she was shocked to her core, mortified with embarrassment, even. But he was confident that initial response would soon evaporate, to be replaced by the lust he knew lurked just beneath her very proper and innocent veneer. Lady Frances De Whytte was, at heart, a strumpet. He meant to bring out those finer qualities in his delightful new bride.

He thrust his tongue as far inside her entrance as he could, then withdrew to slowly trace the lips again. He repeated his penetration, making a point of his tongue and driving it as deep as he was able while Frances writhed and thrashed on the mattress. He supposed she was trying to remain still, but it pleased him to see that she was failing so badly, no more able to control her response than she could manage not to breathe.

He withdrew his tongue, only to replace it with one long finger. He kept the strokes unhurried. It was vital that she should not be hurt or unduly frightened. A little healthy trepidation was quite another matter, however.

He shifted slightly and used the fingers of his free hand to peel back the fleshy hood concealing all but the tip of her most sensitive spot He blew on the exposed nubbin. Frances stiffened. Before she had a chance to register her surprise, he took the engorged flesh between his lips and sucked.

She screamed.

He paused, looked up at her. "Is there a problem, my darling?"

"What…? What did you do?"

"Do you mean this?" He took the plump bud into his mouth again, this time scraping his teeth across the tip, then flicking it with his tongue.

Her fingers were in his hair, all attempts to cling to the headboard seemingly forgotten. He might punish her for that. Later.

Richard sucked again and slid a second finger into her snug channel. He curled his fingers, applying pressure to that spot within, as though seeking to stroke her most sensitive nubbin from the inside. He knew the instant he found the exact spot because Frances made a sound deep in her throat, and her entire body contracted when her orgasm overwhelmed her.

It was not her first climax at his hands, but he was ready to wager that he had surpassed his previous endeavours. Frances continued to spasm and shake, tugging on his hair as though to press her sensitive nubbin harder against his mouth. She was greedy, grasping, drinking in the joy of the experience. Her inner muscles convulsed, too, clamping down hard around his questing fingers. The ripples of her release continued for several moments after she eventually lay still on the mattress, her mouth slack, her breathing heavy.

Richard took his weight on his elbows. He drew his fingers from her and dropped a kiss on her mound, then moved up the bed to plant a deeper kiss on her mouth.

Frances slid her fingers back into his hair. She parted her lips and sucked his tongue inside. Could she taste herself on him, he wondered? Surely she must.

His cock, meanwhile, had arrived at a state way beyond impatient. His balls ached. He would explode if he did not have her. Now.

He released the ties on his breeches to free his swollen erection, then rested his forehead on hers. "Sweetheart, I need to be inside you."

"I know. I… My grandmother told me… She explained about the duties of a good wife."

"I want you to forget anything that anyone may have told you about duty, and just trust me."

"I do. I will. I… I want this, too."

Aye, he was sure enough that she did, even if 'this' remained, for now, a somewhat vague concept. Not for much longer, though. Richard shifted again, intending to position himself between her legs, but then thought better of it.

"Roll over," he commanded. "Onto all fours."

"All fours? But I thought…"

The dowager's influence, doubtless. He meant to surprise her even more before he was done. "Yes. Quickly, if you would."

Obedient, she wriggled out from beneath him and turned over to lie facedown.

"On your knees. Lift up your bottom. I am sure you remember how."

She blanched at the recollection. "Please, you do not mean to spank me...? Why? Have I done something to displease you?"

"No, my sweet. No spanking today. I have something even more... exquisite in mind for you." He waited until she arranged herself in the exact position he required, then he raised the hem of her shift to expose her perfect, heart-shaped bottom. "Spread your thighs, Frances. I need your knees to be wide apart and your lovely arse high. Show me your cunny. Show me how wet and ready you are."

"I am not... I mean, you should not say such things. It is not seemly."

He delivered a light slap to her buttock, enough to remind her of the vulnerability of her situation, but nowhere near hard enough to hurt.

"I thought you said—"

"Did I hurt you?"

"No, but—"

"When I mean you to squeal, you will know it. Settle down now and enjoy what I have planned for you."

"Y-yes, my lord."

His cock leapt to attention. Christ, he could wait no longer. He grasped the shaft of his erection in his fist, pumped up and down twice, hard, then placed the bulbous, weeping head at her entrance. He used his fingers to part her lips and arrange them around the crown of his cock, in readiness for her to receive his first thrust.

"You are a virgin, so there will be pain at first. But it will be swift, and fleeting, and you will accept it without complaint."

"Yes, my lord. My grandmother mentioned that." She shifted her exquisite backside and actually tried to push back as though she might engulf his cock of her own volition. "Is this an occasion when I am meant to squeal?"

Richard made a mental note to permit her to lower herself onto his erection at some point soon, and he would allow her to dance there to her heart's content. But on this occasion, he would take the lead.

"Aye, you may cry out if you feel the need." He rocked his hips to ease his cock a little deeper, then deeper still until he came up against the unmistakable inner barrier. He had two choices now. He could continue with firm but gentle insistence until her maidenhead succumbed, or he could deliver the single powerful thrust which would bury him balls-deep in her channel.

The choice made, he flexed his hips, then drove his cock forward to fill her.

"Aaaagh!" Frances let out a keening moan, and her body went rigid. Her small fist grasped the sheet beneath her. She shook. "Please, Richard…"

"Hush, my darling. It is over. No more pain." He wrapped his arms around her to cup her breasts and weighed their lush fullness. Her swollen nipples pebbled between his fingers as he squeezed and tugged on them. The distraction settled her, as he had hoped it would.

She arched her back, pressing her breasts into his palms.

Slowly, with the utmost care, he withdrew half his length, then drove his cock balls-deep again.

"Oh," she gasped. "Oh."

"Better?" He kissed her neck.

She nodded.

Richard repeated the unhurried, even thrust. Her channel was slick, the wet heat of her inner walls caressing his length. She was tight, so snug she might have been sculpted especially for him. It crossed Richard's mind that this may well be what paradise felt like, and if it was, he would meet his Maker with a smile on his face.

This delight could not last long, but he was determined to show her pleasure once more before he left his

132

seed within her. She needed to know, beyond any doubt, that their bed sport was for both of them, not just for his gratification.

Her grandmother may have spoken to her of duty. He would teach her about passion and desire and pure, wicked, wondrous lust.

He pulled back again, almost completely out of her this time. When he speared his cock back in, it was hard and fast and as deep as this wonderfully accommodating position would permit. Frances groaned and squeezed her inner muscles to caress the length of his shaft.

"I can be gentle, but I do not wish to be."

"I… I do not believe I wish it, either."

"If I hurt you, you will tell me."

"Yes," she murmured. "But you will not."

He dropped another kiss on her neck, then straightened to kneel upright behind her. He watched, entranced, took his time withdrawing his cock, then plunged it deep again. Her body opened to accept him, and he loved the sight of his thick cock disappearing into her channel. He traced the outline with his fingers, then eased his hand around to the front to rest the tip of his middle finger on her sensitive bud. Now, each time he moved, his finger dragged across the tender button, creating a new rush of sensation for her. At the same time, he angled his thrusts to apply pressure to that most receptive spot within her body.

Frances writhed in pleasure. She rolled her hips, tightened her channel around him, and thrust back to meet his driving penetration with an enthusiasm almost equal to his own.

Jesus, I cannot hold back…

He took her nubbin between his fingers and pinched it hard, then rammed his greedy cock as deep as he was able and held still.

His erection jerked violently.

Frances let out another keening yowl, the instant before her release sent her body into shivering convulsions.

Richard's balls twisted, contracted painfully. "Fuck," he shouted. "Fuck, fuck, fuck."

Ribbons of hot seed shot upwards and out to fill his bride's welcoming channel.

Minutes later, the sky outside now completely dark, Richard drifted off to sleep with his bride in his arms. Her rounded bottom was tucked neatly against his lower abdomen, and his softening cock nestled between her buttocks. They were, as he had thought, a perfect fit.

Chapter Twelve

"Must you go?" Frances draped her arms about her husband's neck. "Could your trip not wait until the weather is more clement? I fear it may snow before the day is out, and it is so much warmer here in our bed."

Richard kissed her, then stood upright. He was already dressed, his sword belt at his waist, his fur-lined cloak over his arm. "I fear not, my love, inviting though the prospect might be. There is no need for you to leave our bed at this hour, though." He strode across the chamber to hurl another log into the fireplace then bent to stir the embers into a promising blaze. "Plymouth is not that far, and I shall be home by nightfall, or by tomorrow at the latest."

"If you do not return this evening, that will be the first time we have been apart at night since our wedding," Frances observed, not especially enamoured of the prospect. In the two weeks since they had been wed, she had learned most thoroughly the joys of sharing her bed with a man who was both inventive and skilled as a lover. Generous, too, if somewhat demanding. She did not believe she would have him any other way.

"A whole fortnight," he agreed. "You will keep the bed warm for me, my lady?"

"If I must, but try to return tonight if you can. I... I shall miss you."

"And I shall miss you, too, but you know as well as any that I may not neglect my duty. The king's business requires my presence in Plymouth, so I must go." He returned to the bed to drop another kiss on her mouth, then strode for the door.

She knew he was right, but that did not mean she had to like it. Frances lay back against the pillows until the sound of horses reached her from the courtyard outside. She rushed to the window to open the shutters and caught a final glimpse of her husband, accompanied by his brother and four armed guards, cantering across the drawbridge. Within minutes, they were out of sight.

Frances sniffed at the frigid air. It was still only

135

December, and the worst of the winter had yet to come, but already the early morning felt laden with snow. Heavy dark clouds glowered and a brisk wind cast an even greater chill over the countryside. She shivered, slammed the shutters closed again, and scuttled back to the bed.

She could not huddle beneath the sheets forever. Richard was not the only one with duties to attend to. Frances spent the morning with her grandmother. Together, they sorted linens and set aside the lighter fabrics to be stored somewhere dry over the winter months. The heavier blankets they inspected for signs of wear or damage before having Sara and a couple of other maidservants take them to the various bedchambers. By the time they finished the task and called for their midday meal to be brought to the dowager's chamber, the first flurries of snow had started to fall.

Frances' heart sank. She knew that snow did not bode well for her husband's early homecoming. She would probably sleep alone tonight.

Lady Margaret laid her hand over Frances' fingers. "Do not fret, my dear. He will be back by tomorrow."

"I know. It is just…"

"I understand. And I am pleased to see that you appear to have become reconciled to this marriage of yours."

"Richard is… not as I expected."

The dowager chuckled. "Your expectations were low, child, which makes your fortitude in accepting the match even more commendable. Mine were high, and thus far the lad has not failed to live up to them. I am glad to see you happy. You deserve to find contentment. And security."

Frances allowed herself a wry smile. None but her grandmother would dare to refer to their powerful new duke as 'the lad'.

"Thank you. I believe that I have found both, and I am under no illusions regarding how fortunate I am."

The old woman gazed into the flickering flames in the hearth. "I, too, found such contentment with your grandfather, though it was not to last. As you know, my husband fell at St Alban's thirty years ago, fighting for the sixth King Henry.

136

You are fortunate indeed that those vicious hostilities are at an end."

"I understand that, but—"

"No buts, Frances. War leaves far too many widows in the wake of men's glory. Now, we should—"

The dowager paused when a soft knock sounded at the door to her chamber.

"Enter," she called out.

Sara appeared in the doorway and dropped a hasty curtsy. "My lady, you are needed in the kitchens."

"The kitchens?" Lady Margaret made to rise. "Could not Mrs Lark attend me here if she needs to speak with me?"

"No, my lady. I meant, 'tis Lady Frances who is needed."

Frances patted her grandmother's hand. "Mrs Lark probably wants to consult me regarding how many to expect for the evening meal tonight. I will be back shortly." She followed Sara from the room and headed towards the stairs which led down to the kitchens.

"My lady, I…"

Frances paused to regard the maid. "Sara? Is there a problem?"

"It… it is not the kitchens where you are needed, my lady."

Frances raised an eyebrow. "Indeed? Then where?"

"I… You see…" the girl stammered.

Frances strode back to where Sara stood. "You are starting to worry me now. Tell me what has happened."

"M-my brother… Donald…"

"Is he in some sort of danger again? I swear, trouble follows that lad."

Sara shook her head. "No, 'tis not him, not this time. But he was out, as always, exploring and poking about where he should not be… and he found…"

"What did your brother find, Sara?" Frances pressed. An awful thought struck her. "Is it the duke? My husband?

"No. I mean, yes. The duke. The other duke. Your brother…"

Confusion and relief warred. Frances shook her head

in an attempt to clear her thoughts. "Edmund? What of him? Did Donald discover some clue as to his whereabouts?"

Oh, dear Virgin, do not let him have been killed. Or captured...

"Not that, my lady. Donald found your brother. He has been injured and he needs help."

"Edmund? Injured? Where?" Frances was already striding for the outer door.

"Wait, my lady. Your cloak, and boots. I have them ready... by the fire."

Frances halted. Sara was right, it would not do to set off into the snow without suitable attire. She rushed over to the settle by the fireplace and started to tug on her boots. Sara knelt to assist, then hastily donned her own pair of outdoor shoes.

"You mean to come with me?" Frances asked. "I cannot allow that. It would be too dangerous. My husband..."

"You will need me to show you where he is, my lady."

The maid's features were set in a determined expression, and Frances had to confess she would appreciate her company and her aid. "Very well." She pulled her thick winter cloak about her shoulders, and Sara did the same. Together, they hurried out into the now thickening snow.

"Where is he?" Frances asked, her head bent low to avoid the bite of the wind.

"In the trees," Sara replied, "close to the river."

And close to the entrance to the secret tunnel. Was Edmund perhaps hoping to sneak back into Castle Whitleigh?

"We must hurry. This weather will only get worse. He will need shelter, a place to hide until..."

Until what? Frances' plans went no further than finding her brother and dealing with his most immediate needs. The rest must wait.

No more words were exchanged until they reached the thick stand of trees which ran along the riverbank for perhaps a mile. The woodland was dense, the undergrowth even more so. It was an excellent place to hide, but not in the depths of winter. Edmund would freeze to death if they did not get him into the warmth soon.

Frances heard the low murmur of voices ahead and stopped.

"That is Donald," Sara explained. "After he found Sir Edmund he ran home to seek help. I was at the cottage, visiting my mother. I told him to come back here with food and ale, then wait for us."

Frances nodded and approached with caution. She let out a low cry when she caught her first glimpse of her brother. It was a wonder that young Donald had even recognised him, let alone run to get help. A less stout-hearted lad would have fled screaming.

Edmund had clearly not fared well since last she saw him. He had obviously not shaved since the day he left Castle Whitleigh. His beard, long, unkempt, shrouded his features but did little to disguise his sunken cheeks and bloodshot eyes. He had never been a large man, but now his clothes hung from his narrow frame. His hair had grown, too, and flopped lank and dirty about his thin shoulders.

Donald was attempting to entice him to eat, but Edmund showed scant interest in the hunk of bread and cheese offered, despite the obvious fact that he had not eaten for days, perhaps even weeks. Were it not for the occasional groan or flicker of movement, Frances might have almost believed him to be dead already. He looked about as close to it as she ever imagined a person could get and still draw breath.

She dropped to her knees beside him with a strangled cry. "Dear God, what has happened to you?"

Edmund spared her an unfocused glance but offered nothing more.

"Where are you injured, brother?"

It was Sara who answered. "Donald told me he was bleeding from his side."

The lad nodded brightly. "Aye, he was. I stuffed a towel over it, like you told me." He pointed to the lump under the tattered tunic. "Just there. See?"

Frances gently lifted the torn leather and the undershirt, then removed the wadded-up towel in order to inspect the damage. She recoiled in shock. The wound was gaping, clearly infected, and if she was not very much mistaken, she had just caught a glimpse of her brother's bowels.

"It… it needs to be cleaned and dressed. It is a wonder he is not already raging with fever," she managed, decidedly nauseous

"He was rambling a bit, my lady, when I first came across him. That was how I knew he was here…" Donald imparted his news with a cheerful grin, clearly enjoying the day's adventure immensely.

"I see. Yes. Thank you." Frances chewed on her lip as she pondered the best course of action now. "We need to get him inside. The castle or… or perhaps one of the cottages. Who can we trust?"

Sara shrugged. "I do not know. I would have said my mother, especially as she has skills in healing. But since the new duke rescued our Donald, well, she's been singing his praises to all who will listen. I doubt she would go against him."

Frances had thought as much. It was a pity as they could badly do with Betsy Tinker's basket of herbal remedies and skill with a needle just now. Sadly, the same could probably be said for most of the villagers and household staff. Richard had managed to find favour with everyone, and whilst none would wish Edmund ill exactly, neither would they betray the new duke.

How quickly loyalties had shifted.

"The castle, then," Frances decided. "We will need to carry him through the tunnel."

"Tunnel?" Sara regarded her with a puzzled expression. "What tunnel?"

"I expect my wife is referring to the tunnel through which her brother escaped, all those weeks ago."

Frances whirled around to meet the hard, dark gaze of the husband she believed safely away in Plymouth for at least the rest of the day.

"I… I…" She rose to her feet and stood between her

husband and her brother as though she might even now shield Edmund from the wrath of the Tudors. "How did you...?"

Richard ignored her question. "Do I at last have the honour of meeting the elusive Sir Edmund de Whytte?" he enquired mildly, tilting his head to gain a better view of the helpless figure on the ground. "And not before time."

"You will not harm him." Frances squared up to her husband. "I shall not permit it."

"Permit it?" He raised one sardonic eyebrow. "You are under the impression that you wield some power here, perhaps? What has given you that idea, my lady?"

"Edmund is my brother, and—"

"And now my prisoner," Richard completed her sentence.

"How did you find us?" she demanded, not that it really mattered.

"I received word that your brother had been sighted a few miles west of Plymouth and that he was coming in this direction. He had been in custody, I gather, but escaped, though not without a skirmish. I see that he did not come out of that confrontation unscathed."

"He has been gravely injured. He requires proper care, and... and..."

Richard re-sheathed his sword, having seemingly arrived at the conclusion that his quarry offered no threat. "We picked up his trail early this morning, which led us to this spot. I confess, I did not expect to find you at his side, Frances, and I must say your presence here puzzles me. Am I to surmise that you have been in contact with your brother all along and were expecting his arrival?"

"No! Of course not. I... received word, as you did."

"From whom?"

"I cannot say." She tipped up her chin, determined not to land her loyal servants in trouble, too.

Richard spared a glance at Donald, who reddened beneath his gaze, then at Sara. "You do not need to say, my darling, since it is quite plain who brought word to you. But now you may safely leave this matter in my hands. You will go back to Whitleigh at once and wait for me there."

Frances shook her head. "No. I will not leave him with you. He needs to be cared for, his wounds treated. He deserves that much, at least."

"I shall determine what your brother does or does not deserve. And be assured I shall do the same for you, my lady, and for any other members of our household who remain in any doubt as to where their loyalty is owed."

Sir Stephen, who had observed the proceedings in silence up to now, stepped forward to speak to his brother in a low tone.

Frances could not hear what passed, but Richard's response was a curt nod. "It seems I may leave the suitable chastisement of your maid to my brother since he has kindly volunteered for that task. Now go."

She would have protested further, but Richard raised an arm to summon the four guards who she had watched ride across the Whitleigh drawbridge with him that morning. They advanced and, at their commander's muttered instruction, two of then took Frances by the elbows and the other two seized Sara.

"You will return to where the horses are tethered. Take your mounts and escort the duchess and her maidservant back to the castle. Make sure they are kept secure until my brother and I return." Richard lowered himself onto his haunches to better study the injured man. "By the looks of this one, we will not need to trouble ourselves with finding an executioner anytime soon."

"Richard, please... I beg you..."

Her pleas were ignored. Despite her struggles, Frances was no match for the two burly guards and found herself bundled through the trees and out of the woodland. She and Sara were hoisted up into the saddle of one of the horses, though the reins were retained by the guard whose mount had been commandeered and who led the procession back to the castle. Frances was still pleading with them to let her go as the guards escorted her through the great hall, attracting several perplexed looks from the servants. Her husband's men marched her up the stairs to the bedchamber she shared with

142

Richard and pushed both Frances and Sara inside. The sound of the lock turning and the guards' retreating footsteps was the last sound Frances heard before she flung herself, sobbing, onto the bed.

Hours passed. The thin afternoon sunlight gave way to dusk, then darkness. Still, her husband did not present himself in their chamber. Frances resorted to pounding on the door, demanding to be let out, but to no avail. Eventually, Sara persuaded her to lie down on the bed, and she drifted, at last, into a fitful sleep.

She shot bolt upright when the door at last opened. It was still pitch-dark, but she recognised the silhouette of Sir Stephen in the doorway.

"Where is my husband?" she demanded. "And what has happened to my brother?" She began to scramble from beneath the blankets.

"Richard is still… occupied," came the response. "His instructions are that you remain here. As for you…" His gaze shifted to Sara who had been sleeping in the chair close to the fire. "You are to accompany me. Now."

Frances placed herself between Sara and the stern knight. "No. I shall not allow this. Sara is to stay here. I… I need her…"

Sir Stephen was unmoved. He beckoned to Sara, who slid obediently from her chair.

"Sara, wait…"

"I shall be all right, my lady." Sara's voice shook as she scurried past Frances, despite her attempt to reassure her mistress.

"If you hurt her, I shall… I shall…"

"Goodnight, Lady Frances." Sir Stephen bowed his head and gestured for Sara to precede him from the room.

"Wait! I insist that you…" Frances fell silent. She was shouting at a closed, locked door.

Alone in the chamber, she found it impossible to sleep any more. She paced the floor from the door to the window and back again and did not cease even when the first fingers of a grey dawn crept around the closed shutters.

Frances bent to select a log from the pile always kept beside the hearth and tossed it onto the fire. The flames crackled merrily but did nothing to warm her.

It was fully light before the lock turn again, and the door opened. This time, her husband's broad frame filled the doorway.

Frances glared at him. "I insist that you let me out of here. You have no right—"

"On the contrary, my lady, I have every right since I am master here. However, you are now free to leave the bedchamber if you so desire. First, though, there are matters I must discuss with you."

"Ah, yes. Matters. By which you will no doubt mean your determination to beat me for attempting to lend aid to my brother." She narrowed her eyes at him. "That is your usual method, is it not? Well, on this occasion you are wasting your time. You may beat me senseless, but know this, Richard, I would do exactly the same thing again."

Her husband quirked his lip. "I would expect no less of you, Frances. Your boundless loyalty to your family is one of your finest qualities. I have always admired that about you."

"Then, why would you punish me for it?"

"I have no intention of doing so. Unless of course you count a night confined to your chamber…"

"You do not mean to spank me?"

He strolled across the chamber to open the shutters, then leaned against the sill as he faced her, his arms folded. He shook his head. "No, I do not. Had I found myself in similar circumstances I daresay I would have behaved just as you did. I cannot fault you for going to him and wishing to ease his suffering."

"But I do not understand…"

"I have now heard Sara's account of yesterday's events and I am satisfied that you had no prior knowledge of your brother's intention to return here. No one did. He was discovered by chance before he could gain entry to the tunnel. Young Donald is but a child, and he did what came naturally to him when he discovered an injured man in the woods — he ran home to seek help. Sara should have reported de Whytte's presence to me, but since I was absent from the castle it was not entirely unreasonable that she came to you instead. Given that, I expect my brother will deal more leniently with her than he originally intended."

"He must not harm her. She—"

"Frances," he warned. "Let that go. Sara's situation is not something you can affect. It is in Stephen's hands. He has a fondness for the girl, so I expect she will survive reasonably well."

Relief flared, to be replaced by abject despair. "My brother? Is he…?"

"Edmund lives still. He is in my custody."

"Where is he? I must see him. You cannot deny me that, my lord." Her voice hitched. Tears coursed down her cheeks. Frances was ready to plead now.

"I have no intention of denying you any such thing. I shall take you to him."

"Now? I must see him at once."

"Very well. Come." Richard strode to the door, then waited, his hand outstretched.

Chapter Thirteen

He half expected her to refuse to take his hand, but she did not. Her fingers were cold, and her tiny palm seemed so fragile in his. Her grief and despair were almost palpable. In that moment Richard would have offered up his dukedom if he could spare her the inevitable anguish to come. Instead, he settled for linking his fingers with hers and led her from their chamber.

When she would have headed for the main staircase, he paused. "No. We will take the back stairs."

Frances glanced at him but merely shrugged and followed. He guided her to the narrow spiral staircase usually reserved for the servants. It led down to the corner of the great hall, and from there a stone flagged passageway gave access to the kitchens, the hall itself, and the ante-room now occupied by Lady Margaret.

"Why are we coming this way?" Frances asked. "Surely, the quickest way to the guardroom is across the courtyard."

He did not answer. Their destination would be clear soon enough. He checked that no one was using the flagged passageway then hurried her along it, pausing outside the door leading to the dowager's private accommodation. Richard raised his hand to knock.

"Who is there?" a small voice enquired.

"Sir Richard," he replied.

The lock grated, and Frances peered at him in puzzlement. Her grandmother did not usually find it needful to lock her door. The door swung open a crack, and young Donald peeped out.

"Oh, 'tis you, my lord." He opened the door a little wider, just enough to permit the pair of them to enter.

"Good lad. You are doing well." Richard slipped inside, tugging Frances behind him. At the last moment, he took the precaution of covering her mouth with his hand and bent to murmur in her ear, "It is vital that you remain silent, Frances."

She stiffened and would have fought him. He recognised the exact moment she registered the scene within the chamber.

Edmund, the disgraced and disinherited duke of Whitleigh, lay motionless in the old lady's bed. He was barely breathing. His ashen features appeared even more pallid against the rich cream hue of the pillow. Beside him, the dowager perched on a chair, a damp cloth in her hand. She gently mopped her grandson's brow, never even looking up as they entered. Only when he heard the door close and lock behind them did Richard release Frances.

She let out a small cry and ran to the bed. "Edmund. Edmund…" She grabbed his hand and kissed his limp fingers, then leaned over to peer into his face.

Edmund lay absolutely still. Silent as death. Richard had witnessed such pallor before and did not anticipate that the young man was long for this world. His passing would simplify matters considerably, but Richard knew that to lose her brother for a second time, and with such finality, would cause his wife profound grief. He genuinely ached for her.

Frances blinked back at him over her shoulder. "How… how did he get here? I do not understand…"

Richard could explain that, at least. "Stephen and I carried him through the tunnel, ably assisted by young Donald here who kindly led the way and held the torch for us."

"But… why? I thought…"

"I know what you thought." Richard stepped closer and shrugged. "It is simple enough, really. I, too, have a brother. And now, I have a wife."

"You… helped him. For me?"

"I love you. I could do no less."

"But the king…?"

"Henry must never learn of this. Apart from Stephen, and Sara, those of us in this room are the only ones who know of your brother's presence here, and so it must remain. As for helping him…" Richard paused, considered what to say next, but opted for the truth. "I suspect Edmund is beyond anyone's help now. I wish it were not so, but at least this way he will meet his end surrounded by those who love him. And you will be able to say your goodbyes."

Frances let out a despairing sob. "But we must tend him. You will allow that?"

"Of course. Do what you can for him." Richard did not believe for a moment that even the most diligent and skilled nursing would change the inevitable outcome, but he understood his wife's determination to try and would not stand in her way.

He had done what he could, little enough though it was, and now wanted nothing more than to be elsewhere. He had witnessed enough death on the battlefield and had no stomach for standing by and watching another man's life ebb away. "I have other matters requiring my attention so I trust you will excuse me."

Frances nodded, her gaze never leaving her brother's pale features. "Of course. And... thank you."

Back in the hall, Richard drew in a lengthy sigh. He had taken a massive risk, he and Stephen both, but they had been in agreement. Loyalty to their monarch had become embroiled in something else altogether more personal. The situation was complex, sensitive, and likely to end in tragedy whatever course they took. From the moment they came upon the scene out in the woods, they had no choice.

Richard's first concern had been secrecy. He had commanded all four guards to return to the castle, when just two would have been sufficient to ensure that Frances and Sara did as he had instructed. But he required no witnesses to what was to come next.

The moment they were alone, he and Stephen had lifted the unconscious man and carried him to the entrance to the tunnel. Mercifully, it was close by, and they were able to locate it without too much difficulty. Involving young Donald was another risk, but necessary. He had lit their way, but despite this their progress had been slow and stumbling. On more than one occasion as they crept through the darkness, Richard was convinced their man was already dead. Miraculously, Edmund survived the short but difficult journey, and they found themselves at the bottom of the scullery stairs.

Again, Donald proved his worth. The lad slipped ahead to ensure that no one was around to witness their surreptitious arrival. As soon as he whistled, their signal that it was safe to proceed, Richard and Stephen wasted no time in carrying the limp body up the stairs and across the hall.

The choice of the dowager's chamber was the most obvious one since Lady Margaret could be relied on to keep the secret, and she would be able to assist the wounded man. At the very least, Edmund would be comfortable, warm, and dry in his final hours. In the circumstances, that would have to do.

As soon as they deposited their burden in the dowager's bed, much to the old lady's astonishment, and gained her cooperation in the matter, they had crawled back through the tunnel to recover their mounts. Eventually they returned to Whitleigh through the front gates. By then, several hours had elapsed since the guards had been dismissed, so it was not difficult to convince the young captain that the prisoner had expired in the woods. They led him to believe that the duke and his brother had set off to take Edmund de Whytte's remains to Plymouth. However, they had encountered a body of His Majesty's troops on the way and handed the dead man to them to complete his final journey.

All in all, Richard considered their tracks well enough covered. There would, of course, be the final complication of disposing of the body once Edmund did succumb to his wounds, but they could address that when the time came. The main thing, for now, was that Richard would not be compelled to spend the next several decades regaining some measure of peace with his wife. His conscience was clear.

Well, clear enough. Henry may not view it in the same way, but Richard had always maintained that the best a man might manage was to deal adequately and effectively with the situation before him. He had done his best, and now he wished the unfortunate young man in the dowager's bed a speedy and merciful end in the comforting bosom of his family.

It was close to midday when Richard again tapped on the door to the dowager's chamber. Donald let him in. The scene within was almost identical to that he had left hours before, except that now Sara was present also.

"How is he?" Richard enquired.

"There is no change." Frances turned her tear-streaked features towards him. "We have cleaned and dressed his wound, but the fever will not abate."

Richard nodded. He was not surprised at the news, and there was little enough to be said. It was usually the ensuing fever which took the lives of those injured in battle rather than their wounds themselves.

"He has taken a little water," Frances added, "but he will not eat."

"I see."

"I am no healer. Neither is Grandmêre."

It would make no difference anyway. Richard was convinced of that.

"We need Betsy," Frances announced. "Sara's mother. She has knowledge of herbs, and she might—"

"No. No one else must know of this." On that point, at least, Richard was adamant.

"But Betsy can be trusted. She is loyal…"

"To the previous duke, maybe." Richard shook his head. "It is out of the question. I am sorry."

"No, my lord." It was Sara who spoke now. "My mother was loyal to the previous duke, that is true. But not now. Not since you saved our Donald. She would help us, I know it, but only if the request came from you."

"From me?" Richard scowled at the maid. "You must be mistaken, lass."

"I am not, my lord. I swear it. There is nothing my mother would not do for you. If you were to ask her to keep this secret, not a word would ever pass her lips."

"Please, Richard. Please, ask her…" his wife begged.

Richard had his doubts, but his wife's stricken expression did much to dispel them. And after all, whether Betsy Tinker did this thing for him or for her previous lord was immaterial really, as long as she could be relied upon to keep her mouth shut. And if it came to it, whose word would be believed? That of the Duke of Whitleigh, a favourite of the king himself and a battle-scarred hero, or a peasant woman from the village? It was another risk, but one worth taking if it helped to alleviate Frances' distress.

"Very well. I shall talk to her." He bowed and left the women to their ministrations.

He had to enlist the aid of his brother since Richard was not certain which cottage was occupied by the Tinker family. Stephen accompanied him there, then waited outside while Richard entered the tiny dwelling. The woman took little enough convincing regarding the need for secrecy, and agreed to accompany him to the castle, her basket of herbal remedies on her arm.

"If the wound is dressed already, there is nothing more to be done there. 'Tis the fever we must tackle," she announced, piling sprigs of hemlock, henbane, and opium poppies into her basket. "These will help with the pain."

Privately, Richard considered the combination of poisons were more likely to finish the job started by the weapon which had sliced open the previous duke's abdomen, but he said nothing.

"Angelica and chamomile," Betsy added, selecting the herbs from a range of jars on a shelf, "for the fever." Thus prepared, she hurried from the cottage, Richard in her wake.

"It is vital that you are not seen entering Lady Margaret's quarters," Richard reminded her. "We do not wish to arouse suspicion or attract unnecessary questions."

"Yes, yes," Betsy agreed, "though matters might be a great deal simpler if the lad were to be moved to my cottage. I could tend him better then, and we could tell people that it was me who was ailing, or Donald. None would consider it amiss if Lady Frances were to visit regularly, and Lady Margaret, too."

Richard considered this proposal for several moments. "Very well, though I would not recommend moving him now. If he survives this night, we can look to that tomorrow."

Frances slipped into her seat at his right hand when the evening meal was served. The dowager remained in her chamber. By now it was generally understood that the young duchess's brother had met his end the previous day in the woods, so her forlorn expression elicited sympathy rather than surprise. Richard hugged her and bent to murmur in her ear.

"How does he fare?"

"There has been no change," she whispered. "Betsy administered a potion, and I do not believe he is in any discomfort now, but his fever remains."

Richard merely nodded and shoved their shared trencher in front of her. "Eat. You must retain your own strength if you are to assist him."

"I am not hungry."

"Frances," he warned, "you will eat."

She did as he asked, though with not the slightest enthusiasm. He did not argue when she rose quickly from the table and returned to her grandmother's room.

Frances would have remained at her brother's bedside all night if he let her, but that would not do. It would be noticed, suspicions aroused. Richard collected her on his way to their bedchamber and insisted she accompany him there.

"Please, I must stay here. He will need me…"

Richard was not to be dissuaded. "Lady Margaret will be here, and Sara, too. You will be summoned if there is any change."

"But—"

"Frances, you will join me in our bed. Now."

Faced with no choice, she tore herself away and followed him up the narrow spiral stairs again. "I shall not sleep a wink," she complained.

He did not doubt it, but appearances must be maintained, for everyone's sake. In the event, though, exhaustion overcame her, and he was obliged to remove her shoes and draw the blanket over her, then slide into the bed at her side.

When he awoke, he was alone. The first slivers of daylight played around the shutters as he rekindled the fire and splashed cool water onto his face. His first stop after he descended into the hall was to call on the dowager.

Lady Margaret and Frances were alone with Edmund. Sara and her mother had left at first light to get some sleep themselves, and young Donald had gone with them even though he had slept most of the night already.

Richard wondered if, just possibly, the young man looked slightly less pale.

"He has survived the night," Frances said brightly. "That is a good sign, I think."

A bloody miracle, in Richard's view, though he simply shrugged and leaned over to inspect the patient more thoroughly. He could detect no significant improvement, though neither was the man any worse. "I shall leave you to it," he said. "There are fence repairs required and rents to be collected, so I shall be away for much of the day. Perhaps you will join me again for the evening meal."

Frances nodded, her attention fixed upon the prone body in the bed. "Of course, my lord."

The snow had ceased, though a generous carpet still lay over the meadows. The air was cold and crisp, just the sort of winter's day Richard preferred. Were it not for the pall of death hanging over his family, and the associated complexities of caring for the wounded man whilst keeping his presence a secret, Richard might have actually enjoyed his day. Certainly, he found bandying words with his tenants and sharing a mug of ale at each cottage he visited infinitely preferable to a life on the battlefield.

Yes, he could come to love the life of a country nobleman. There were many who relished the bustle and intrigue of court, but Richard was not one of them. He had had enough excitement for one lifetime and would be content to raise plump cattle and fine crops, not to mention strapping sons should the Good Lord see fit to so bless him.

*****

"Wake up, child."

Frances sat bolt upright, alert instantly. "What? Is

153

there some change?"

"He is stirring," her grandmother whispered. "He is trying to speak."

Edmund is conscious?" Frances flung aside the blanket which had been tucked around her knees to ward off the early morning chill and rushed to the bedside. "Edmund? Can you hear me?"

She clutched at his hand. His eyes remained closed, but she was sure she detected the faintest hint of movement. A fluttering, perhaps…

"Edmund. Squeeze my hand if you can hear me," she pleaded.

For long moments there was nothing. Then, weak but most certainly there, she detected the slightest hint of pressure against her fingers.

"He heard me. He gripped my hand." Frances beamed at her grandmother and Sara who both stood at the foot of the bed. "Truly, he did."

The dowager nodded. "Yes, I know. He opened his eyes a short while ago. Just for a moment."

Frances laid her free hand on her brother's forehead. "It is cool," she breathed, her relief and joy almost overwhelming her. "No fever."

"Has he truly returned to us, from the very depths of the grave itself?" Lady Margaret clasped her hands and muttered a brief prayer of thanks to the Blessed Virgin.

Frances shared her grandmother's sentiments but was more concerned with the immediate need to do what she might to aid her brother's miraculous return from the jaws of death. She poured a mug of cool water and held it to his lips, her free arm around his shoulders to support him. "Drink this," she urged.

His lips parted at her command, and his throat worked as he fought to swallow the drops of water. After a few sips he closed his mouth and slumped back against the pillow.

"Can you hear us?" Frances asked again. "Do not try to speak, just nod. Or raise your hand…"

A few moments passed, but this time when it came,

the signal was clear and unmistakeable. He lifted his right hand and allowed it to drop onto the mattress.

"Edmund, I—"

"Enough for now, my lady." Sara laid her hand on Frances' shoulder. "Let him rest."

The next several hours dragged. Edmund was in a state of not-quite consciousness, stirring every half hour or so to take a few sips of water and occasionally to open his eyes. He responded when spoken to with a tightening of his grip or feeble wave of his hand, his mind and sensibilities returning well in advance of his physical faculties.

It was mid-afternoon, and Frances had begun to doze again when he at last managed to croak his first coherent words.

"Frankie…?"

She shot back to wakefulness. "Edmund? Yes, it is me…"

"Where…?" He slid his eyes to the right, then to the left as though trying to identify his surroundings and failing utterly.

"You are at home, with us. This is Grandmêre's room…"

He furrowed his brow and peered at her. His features betrayed his utter incomprehension.

"The ante-room, off the great hall," Frances explained. "Richard thought it would suit her better, being downstairs…" She trailed off. He was already asleep again.

When next he regained consciousness, Edmund remained awake long enough to take his grandmother's hand and even accepted a few mouthfuls of creamy porridge, highly recommended by Betsy who had been summoned to assist.

"Now that he is awake, the sooner we can get him shifted out of here and down to my cottage, the better, she declared. "Ye must speak wi' the duke about it, my lady."

"Yes, I shall," Frances promised. "As soon as he returns."

It will be dark soon…

Frances reached to close the shutters since it was

155

well-known that the damp humours of the night air were harmful to recuperation. Edmund must be kept warm, encouraged to eat, to drink, to rest and recover his strength. She meant to ensure he had every care and comfort she could manage.

"Who is Richard?"

She whirled. Edmund sat up in the bed, his body propped against the pillows. He regarded her with something akin to his usual intelligent gaze.

"Edmund. You are awake. Properly awake…"

"It seems so." He grimaced as he shifted his weight. "Earlier, you mentioned a Richard…"

She perched on the edge of the bed and laid her palm on his forehead. "Your fever is much abated, and—"

He raised his hand to take her wrist between his fingers. "Frankie, answer me. Who is Richard, and why does he get to determine who occupies which rooms here at Whitleigh?"

"Whatever do you mean?"

"Earlier, you said that Richard moved Grandmêre from her chamber to this one. I ask, on what authority did he do that? Who is Richard?"

Frances swallowed, then turned to address the dowager, and Sara. "Would you leave us, please? I need to speak with my brother."

The dowager inclined her head and made her way to the door. "We shall be close by. Summon us when you are ready, child."

Frances waited until the door closed behind them, then swallowed hard. "Edmund, you have been gravely ill. And away for many weeks prior to that. You need to understand—"

"Just tell me, Frankie."

She nodded and met his quiet gaze. "Richard is — was — the Earl of Romsey. I surrendered Whitleigh to him, as we agreed. He is now Duke of Whitleigh, the king's reward to him for his services during the wars between the cousins as they squabbled over the throne…"

156

"He is master here now, then?"

She nodded. "But you knew this would be the case."

"Aye, I did. He has assumed my title?"

"Yes. And… he is also my husband."

Edmund's eyes widened. "You… wed him?"

She nodded again and chewed on her lower lip. Accepting Richard's proposal had been difficult enough at the time. She had never once anticipated having to explain her decision to her brother.

"He coerced you," Edmund stated dully. "He must have."

Again, Frances shook her head. "He made me an offer, and I accepted it. I could have refused and gone into a nunnery instead."

"Some choice! The lesser of two evils, then?"

"Perhaps, but…"

"But?"

"But, I have not regretted my decision. I… I love him."

Edmund slumped against the pillows and regarded her in silence for several moments.

"You love him?"

She nodded. "I do. I truly do."

"He must be a remarkable individual, this Richard of yours, to bring about such a change of heart."

"He is," she answered simply. "He is a good lord to Whitleigh, and he has been kind to me. And to Grandmêre. We… we thought you were gone for ever, so…"

"But now that I am back?"

A good question indeed, but she did not hesitate with her answer.

"I still love him. And I want you and he to be friends. I do not know how that would come about, but it is what I want."

He shook his head. "I share your bewilderment, Frankie." His eyelids were drooping again, and he was already drifting back to sleep. "How could your Richard, this man who now holds my home, my lands, my title… how could he and I ever be reconciled?"

157

Frances was not about to concede. "Richard rescued you, out there in the woods. He brought you home, to us."

"He did… what?"

"Richard saved you."

"Why…?"

"Because… he loves me."

*****

Dusk was falling when Richard clattered back across the Whitleigh drawbridge accompanied by his men and his brother. He tossed his reins to a groom and headed for the warmth of his hearth. Frances awaited him at the entrance to the hall, and from her expression he surmised that she, too, had had a good day.

She gripped his hand as soon as he entered. "Come, please," she urged.

He loosened his cloak and slung it over his arm, then followed her to the dowager's room where he found Edmund, clearly awake at last, and accepting a few mouthfuls of broth.

"See," Frances whispered, "he is better."

It certainly appeared so. Had matters been complicated before, there were infinitely more so now. A dead Edmund would have been tricky to dispose of, but Richard had no notion whatsoever how he might deal with a live one.

"You have done well," he agreed, his mind still reeling as the implications sank in. "All of you. Betsy is to be commended…"

"It was her fever cure, I am sure of it. He is still very weak, but I do believe he will live." Frances beamed at him, the relief etched in her lovely features.

Inconvenient though this turn of events might be, Richard could not begrudge his wife her joy. "It looks as though he has some way still to go, but you may be right."

"I am, I am quite sure of it. I… I should like you to meet him. Properly."

He supposed that was inevitable. And,he had never seen her happier.

Thus resigned, Richard stepped up to the bed. "Sir Edmund. I am glad to see you looking somewhat better."

Pale-blue eyes returned his gaze. The man's features closely resembled those of his wife, though a masculine form. The ousted duke extended his hand.

"Sir Richard. My sister speaks highly of you."

Richard draped his arm around Frances' shoulders and dropped a kiss on her hair. "You will be aware that your sister and I are now married."

"My felicitations. And, I gather I owe you thanks for my life."

Richard did not answer. Despite appearances, he was not yet convinced that Edmund's life did not still hang in the balance. If his presence here was discovered, the matter would be out of his hands anyway.

"Am I under arrest?" Edmund continued.

Richard gave that some thought. "I think that we had better assume that you are, until a better arrangement might be agreed.

"But there are no locks. No chains, no guards…"

"Let us hope they do not become necessary."

Stephen shared Richard's dismay at the unexpected turn of events. "God's bones, this is not how we imagined this would end. What are we to do now?"

The pair shared a jug of ale in the duke's bedchamber while Richard imparted the change in Edmund de Whytte's condition. Unfortunately, Richard had no ready answer to his brother's perfectly reasonable question. "We must wait and see what transpires. He may yet have a relapse…" Which would likely plummet Frances into an even deeper pit of despair than would have been the case had her brother not survived the night. He could not wish that on her.

"We have to do something. We need to get rid of him."

Richard could not disagree. He took another swig of ale and wondered what the next few days might bring.

On a brighter note, now was probably a good time to

broach the matter of the king's wedding with Frances.

"But, why?" she demanded when he informed her at supper that her presence was expected at their sovereign's marriage celebrations in London. "Why would Henry Tudor want me at his wedding?"

"You are my duchess. It is natural that you would attend, with me."

"Could you not say that I am indisposed?"

"Are you?" he enquired.

"Well, no, but…"

"You are a duchess. You know well enough what that entails. The wedding is in a month's time. We shall journey to London soon after Christmas."

"But I do not have a wardrobe suitable for court." When she resorted to levelling practical objections at him, Richard knew that he had won.

"You have a couple of weeks in which to rectify that matter. Your blue silk will do to start with, and I am sure that you and Sara can achieve whatever else is needed."

"But what about caring for Edmund? And preparing for Christmas?"

More practicalities. "We have a houseful of servants who can hang a few holly sprigs and drag a yule log into our hall. As for your brother, we shall move him tonight, when the castle is all abed, so that Betsy Tinker can do what is needed for him. Your grandmother, too. He will not be neglected."

"But I cannot leave him to spend weeks away at court…"

Now, here was a genuine objection. Richard was ready to concur. They could not leave Castle Whitleigh as long as the previous duke was ensconced in his old home and ready to wreak God only knew what havoc as soon as Richard's back was turned and Edmund was well enough to stagger from his sickbed.

Stephen was right. They had to be rid of this troublesome nobleman who had quite simply refused to die.

Chapter Fourteen

Frances knelt beside her husband in the tiny chapel while the priest from Falstone Priory chanted the words of the Christmas mass. Her Latin was adequate enough, but she did not comprehend all of the service. What she did know was that her knees ached, the chapel was cold, and a delicious feast awaited them back in the hall.

Surely the sweet Christ child will not require a great deal more in the way of devotions...

Richard cleared his throat, a sure sign that he, too, had had enough. Sadly, this particular friar was made of sterner stuff than the priest who had officiated at their wedding, and the signal fell on deaf ears. The assembled household was compelled to endure a full half hour more of rhythmic Latin chanting before the holy father appeared satisfied and bestowed the final blessing upon his restless congregation.

For Frances, the time was not wasted. It afforded her ample opportunity to offer up her own, private appreciation to the Blessed Virgin for restoring her precious brother to her. God and all the saints had been merciful and generous, though she was not unaware of the part played by the man who knelt beside her.

The service concluded, Richard assisted her up off her knees, and Frances staggered slightly as the blood supply was restored to her lower limbs. Richard steadied her, then led her back down the aisle of the chapel and out into the crisp breeze of a frigid Christmas morning. They trooped back into the hall, the household chattering behind them. The delightful aroma of roast swan filled Frances's nostrils, and, if she was not mistaken, a goose, too. It would be slathered in butter and saffron and surrounded by vegetables and nuts. There would be mince tarts, too, a favourite of hers since childhood, baked and crammed with shredded meats, fruits, and spices. The seasonal furmenty would be set out for the villagers, and perhaps a pudding of thick porridge with currants, dried fruits, and eggs, lavishly flavoured with cinnamon.

A yule log burned in the hearth, and there would be carols sung by the villagers once they had filled their bellies.

There might even be mumming, and dancing later, when the feasting was done and the tables cleared aside, though she did not feel much like dancing herself. She was tired of late, the result, no doubt, of caring for Edmund day and night.

Still, her appetite was undiminished, and she did justice to Mrs Lark's fine creations. Richard made sure her trencher was rarely less than half full, and he seemed to know which were her favourite delicacies.

"Have you tried this ham with mustard?"

"You should have some more of the stewed chicken, my love."

"Mrs Lark's gingerbread is even better than the stuff our cook at Keeterly used to make when I was young."

Or he would tempt her with honeyed nuts and heady spiced wine, plum pudding, or perhaps a handful of candied almonds.

Eventually, she could manage no more. "I really should check on Edmund," she whispered.

Her brother had been moved, under cover of darkness, and now resided at the Tinkers' cottage. They had spread the story that Betsy herself was unwell, thus explaining why she was keeping to her home these last couple of weeks. Visitors were discouraged for fear of contagion, and no one argued with that. Disease could spread so rapidly...

The duke and duchess, of course, were honour-bound to see to the welfare of their people, so Frances' regular visits laden with food and other supplies went unremarked. The Christmas celebrations made no difference to that duty, so no one thought it odd that she and Richard would be seen leaving the hall carrying a tray laden with sliced meats and other delicacies.

When they entered the Tinkers' cottage, Edmund was seated at the crude table in the cramped abode playing a game of checkers with Donald. He got to his feet to greet his sister and her husband.

"Sir Richard," he murmured, bowing. "Frankie."

"Edmund," Richard replied. "I trust you are well." If there was an awkwardness to their greeting, no one saw fit to comment.

"He is better with every day that passes," Frances declared brightly. "Is that not so, Betsy?"

The older woman was seated on a low stool beside her fire, stirring a large pot. She nodded. "Aye, the wound has healed well and the fever gone. I reckon he may be near enough good as new."

"And it is thanks to you," Frances continued. "And Sara. And of course, Donald played his part, too. I can never thank all of you enough."

"There is no need, my lady." Betsy got to her feet. "Is that for us?" She eyed the tray of Christmas treats.

"It is, yes." Richard set the tray down beside the checkers board. "You should not miss out on all of the celebrations because you were stuck here, helping us."

Donald took no persuading at all. The game abandoned, he tucked into the seasonal fare whilst the duke and duchess received more detailed reports of Edmund's condition.

"It sounds as though you will soon be well enough to leave," Richard announced quietly.

The room fell silent.

"Leave?" Edmund echoed.

"Yes." Richard met his gaze. "You must realise that you cannot remain here."

Edmund did not argue.

Appalled, Frances looked from her brother to her husband. "What do you mean, Richard? Where would he go?"

"Well," Richard began, only to be interrupted by Edmund who at last found his voice.

"Your husband is correct, Frankie. If I stay here, I will be arrested, and the rest of you with me, as like as not. Nothing has changed. I am still condemned as a traitor, and you would all suffer the same fate if it were known that you aided me."

"I do not care," she insisted.

Edmund smiled wryly. "No, but I would wager your husband does."

"Richard wants what is best. He would not do

163

anything to harm you. Or me."

"No, but that does not mean he wants me around for much longer. Am I right, my lord?"

Frances would have protested further but could only glare when Richard slowly nodded. "Aye. We must think of a way to get you out of here."

"No, Richard. You cannot do this. He is still weak, and—"

"Frankie," Edmund interrupted her, "I am well enough, thanks to your care and that of the others here. I am grateful, grateful enough to know when it would be wrong to impose further on your husband's generosity."

"Richard does not mean it. He will not hand you over to the king, will you?"

"Of course not," Richard replied. "Had that been my intention I would have done it weeks ago."

"See, Edmund? You are welcome here. My husband has said so."

Richard shook his head. "That is not what I said. I have been thinking…"

"Thinking?" Frances paced the tiny room. "What is there to think about?"

"I have been thinking, "Richard continued, addressing his words to Edmund now, "that it would be best for all concerned if you were to leave England."

Edmund nodded. "Frances and I arrived at the same conclusion, my lord. That was my intention when I left here all those weeks ago. Unfortunately, matters did not proceed as I had hoped. I was spotted by Henry's troops when I tried to approach the docks at Plymouth and recognised. You know the rest."

"Well, this time we must do better." Richard scratched his chin, deep in thought. "I shall find out which ships are to leave Plymouth in the coming days, and we will decide on the best choice. I am thinking Spain, and from there you might be able to find passage with one of Queen Isabella's famed exploratory expeditions. Of course, once you leave these shores, you must never return."

"But where might he end up?" Frances gasped. "We will never see him again."

Richard rose and took her in his arms. "Surely you can see, Frances, this is the only way to guarantee his safety. Edmund will be in grave danger for as long as he remains in England. It is only a matter of time until he is discovered, and you know how that will end. This way, if we can manage to get him aboard a suitable ship, he will live. And he will be free."

"But… it is so dangerous."

"No more so than if he should he remain here, surrounded by enemies who would see him executed in a heartbeat." Richard looked to Edmund. "What do you say to this?"

Edmund did not hesitate. "I say 'thank you', my lord. It is an excellent solution, more than I might have hoped for."

Two nights later, Frances, Richard, and Stephen dined alone in the duke's chamber.

"The *Charity* is to leave for Cadiz in five days' time," Stephen informed them. "She is a merchant ship, carrying a cargo of copper, and is in need of crewmen, or so I hear."

"Edmund is no sailor," Frances remarked. "You cannot expect him to swab decks and haul on ropes. I had thought we might purchase a passage for him."

"Then he must learn seamanship," was her husband's terse response. "A paying passenger is much too memorable for my liking, whereas a common sailor will go unnoticed. Five days, you say?"

"Yes. Since you will be on your way to London for the royal wedding, I could see Edmund safe to Plymouth and get him aboard. The ship's master will not ask too many questions as long as his crew are hale and hearty, and we could take the added precaution of slipping him a few shillings to better sweeten the deal."

Richard shook his head. "The king will expect to see you at his wedding as well as us since you will no doubt be eager to thank him for his generosity in awarding Keeterly to you. In my experience it is best not to disappoint insecure monarchs. I have a better idea. We shall all travel to London via Plymouth. We will stay at an inn for the night, and somehow contrive to see Edmund aboard the *Charity* ourselves. My wife shall have the opportunity to take her leave of her brother properly. Then, the rest of us will continue on to court to celebrate Henry's marriage."

Frances considered this suggestion, chewing nervously on her lower lip. "How will we conceal Edmund on the journey? We will have guards with us, surely."

"Richard nodded, deep in thought. "A fair enough question, Frances, especially since all our soldiers believe Edmund to be dead. His sudden resurrection would prove somewhat startling. Still, I am sure I can rely upon you to be traveling with vast amounts of luggage. You will require a stout, sizable chest… or three. To carry all your gowns and whatnot…?"

"You mean to conceal my brother in a chest?"

"I am open to better suggestions, naturally."

None were forthcoming. The matter was settled.

Clad in her linen night rail, Frances curled up in the chair closest to the fire to await her husband. The flames crackled cheerily, and the room was pleasantly warm, despite the December chill outside. Beside her, a goblet of spiced wine also served to keep out the cold. She took a sip, then set the vessel aside when she heard footsteps outside in the corridor.

The door opened, and Richard entered. He glanced her way.

"I had not expected you to still be up. Why are you not tucked up warm beneath the blankets, sweetheart?" He sat on the edge of the bed to remove his boots.

"Please, allow me to help you." Frances scrambled from her perch and scurried to kneel at his feet.

"There is no need. Get into bed where it is warm."

"I am perfectly warm enough, my lord." She unfastened the buckles on his leather boots and tugged off the first one. Richard let her get on with it, and soon the second boot joined the first.

"Such solicitousness is not like you, my love."
Richard frowned at her. "Not that I object, of course. But I
cannot help wondering… has something happened?"

"No. I mean, yes."

He cupped her chin in his palm. "Which is it?"

"I wanted to talk to you, that is all."

"Very well. Say what you need to." He started to
unfasten the buttons on his overtunic.

Frances remained on her knees, watching him
undress. Although they had now been wed for several weeks,
this was a sight she did not tire of. He was a remarkably
handsome man, this one she had married so reluctantly, and
never less so in her opinion than when he was unclothed. No
doubt the holy fathers at Falstone would declare her
fascination with her husband's nude form both wicked and
wanton, but it was not to be helped. She might be destined for
eternal damnation but was nevertheless utterly beguiled by his
muscled physique, the planes and contours of his chest, the
sprinkling of dark hair which traced a tantalising path beneath
his breeches to form a dark nest around his cock.

And what a beautiful cock it was, though she had
nothing against which to make the comparison. It did not
matter to her, there could be no other as wondrous as this.
Already swelling within his breeches, she knew the shaft to be
thick and veined in an intricate pattern, the crown round and
slick. On the rare occasions when she had brushed it with her
hand, the skin felt oddly smooth and silky. It was not what she
had expected, and she longed to make a more thorough
exploration. Perhaps he would permit that since Richard
denied her little in the way of pleasure in their bed.

Her handsome husband possessed not a modest bone
in his body. He disrobed quickly, then, gloriously naked,
strolled across the chamber to pick up the goblet of spiced
wine she had left.

"May I?" He held up the cup.

Frances nodded, and he took a generous drink, then
offered it to her.

"I have had enough, thank you."

He set the goblet down and returned to stand before

her. "You look troubled, sweetheart. Tell me."

"I… I wish to apologise," she began.

He bent to sweep her hair back from her face with a gentle hand. "Why?"

"I… I was unjust."

He raised an eyebrow. "How so?"

She took a deep breath, attempted to assemble her thoughts in some sort of order. In the end, she just blurted out the concerns uppermost in her mind. "When first you came here. I… I hated you so much. I was convinced you were my enemy. I was belligerent and hostile, and I did not trust you. I accused you of so many awful things…"

"As I recall, I *was* your enemy. And some of what happened between us was far from pleasant, though I hope I was never unduly cruel. Still, your animosity was to be expected, and I have never held it against you."

"I know that. I feel so ashamed now. You… you are a far better person than I am."

He dropped to his haunches, so their eyes were on a level. "I have no complaints. Come to bed."

"I want to be a good wife."

"As I have said, I have no complaints on that score."

"You did not have to marry me, but you did anyway. And… I have never thanked you for it."

He sighed. "You do not need to thank me."

"I do. And as for Edmund… he would be dead now, I am quite sure of it, but for you."

"It was Betsy's doing, in the main. And your grandmother's"

"But you made it possible. You brought him here, to his home, where he could be cared for by those who loved him. I know full well you did not expect him to survive, but even so, it was kindly done." She met his gaze. "But I do not understand why you did it. I… I am not sure that I would have done the same had our positions been reversed."

"Ah, so that is it. This is why you consider yourself a lesser person than me."

Frances nodded. "Can you forgive me?"

168

"There is nothing to forgive. You understand the importance of family better than anyone else I know. Our kin are all we have, that and our honour. When you and I were wed, your family became mine. Edmund is your brother, and, by marriage, mine, too. I could do no other than help him when the need arose, and whatever you might think now, however much you might castigate yourself and consider yourself lacking somehow, I know that if the occasion called for it you would have done the same for my brother."

"I would like to think so, but—"

"Enough, Frances. You are my wife. I love you. I mean to devote my life to making you happy, to ensuring that you never regret choosing me over the cloister—"

"As if I would," she exclaimed.

He grinned. "Your obvious distaste for a life of religion, devotion, and prayer is another of your finer qualities. You would have made a dreadful nun."

Emboldened, she reached for his cock and wrapped her fist around it. "I suspect you would fare equally badly as a monk, my lord."

He let out a low groan. "Christ's balls, Frances, that feels good."

She drew her hand along his length. He hardened and swelled under her touch. Frances stretched up to brush her lips over his. "I mean to practice hard at being a good wife, my lord, and a poor nun."

"I am delighted to hear it. And whilst what you are doing right now is, in my view, perfect conduct in a good and dutiful wife, it is likely to result in me tumbling you onto your back, dragging your night rail up to your waist, and fucking you here on the rug."

"As your good and dutiful wife, I do not consider it my place to complain about where you fu… Where you… er…"

His sensuous mouth curled in a wicked smile. "A good wife will always be specific in her answers, when questioned by her husband. Where would you like me to fuck you, Frances?"

"I… you know. You do not need me to say it."

169

"But I wish you to. Be specific, my love. Tell me, what would you like me to do to you here on this sheepskin rug before our roaring fire? Oh, and whilst you are considering that question, please do not stop what you are doing."

Frances tightened her grip on his thick erection and pumped her hand up and down in the manner she has seen him do. Despite her lewd actions, she could still not quite manage to wrap her tongue around the words he desired. "I… I…"

He lowered his forehead to rest on hers. "Christ's blood, Frances, I love you…"

"I love you, too, my lord. And…" She took a deep breath. "And I would love you to fuck me on the rug." There. She had said it. She was truly wicked now and had thus far not been struck down by divine retribution.

Richard seemed to concur. "Since I have clearly had the good fortune to marry a strumpet, can I suggest that you lie back, spread your legs, and we shall be ungodly together?"

Chapter Fifteen
18 January, 1486

"Where do you suppose he is now?" Frances wondered aloud.

Richard did not pretend to misunderstand. "The *Charity* sailed almost a month ago. Edmund should have reached Cadiz by now, provided the weather has not been inclement."

"The winter is such a dangerous time to set sail…"

"Even more dangerous for him to stay. Edmund understood the risks. This was what he wanted."

"I know. But it hurts, knowing I shall never see him again."

Richard draped an arm about her shoulders and drew her to him. "Never is a long time. None of us knows what the future holds. This way, at least, his fate is in his own hands once more. Though I had little opportunity to get to know him well, your brother struck me as a natural adventurer, and I would not be surprised if Edmund manages to do very well for himself. And, he promised to send word, when he could."

"I know. That is something, I suppose." She turned, forced a smile, and wrinkled her nose as she properly inspected his attire. "Did I mention, you look exceptionally fine today, my lord?"

"I believe you may have made such a comment. I am relieved to learn that my efforts have not been in vain, for I would not have wished to be outshone by you, especially on such a grand occasion."

At his suggestion, she had chosen to wear the pale-blue silk to attend the royal nuptials, though now the shimmering fabric was augmented by a pair of sapphire earrings and a matching brooch. Lady Margaret's necklace glittered against her throat. A new, ermine-lined cloak warded off the worst of the January chill.

He brought the hood up to cover her bright curls. "Come, we should take our places in the Abbey. The king will not appreciate us being late for his wedding."

As was befitting for a commander who had played a

major part in helping his monarch to victory at Bosworth, Richard, Duke of Whitleigh, and his duchess had been allocated a place in the middle of the central nave at Westminster Abbey, the most revered church in the land and the only place Henry considered suited to the august occasion of his marriage. They were behind the royal family themselves but in front of less distinguished and favoured subjects. As they made their way to their pews, Stephen nodded to them from his seat only a few rows farther back.

"Will we be expected to meet the king again? I am not sure my nerves will stand it."

Frances had, in Richard's view, managed to carry off her first encounter with her new monarch rather well. They had attended his court immediately after their arrival in London since it would not do to appear tardy, and Frances had been greeted cordially enough. If the king harboured any lingering doubts regarding the loyalties of the new duchess he was gracious enough to leave that fact unremarked. Instead, he allowed her to kneel at his feet, kiss the ring of state, and congratulated her on her recent marriage.

His welcome for Richard himself was rather more effusive, and for Stephen barely any less so. He watched impassively as they bent their knees and bowed their heads, swearing allegiance to him as their true and rightful monarch, then he flung his arms about the pair of them and insisted that they share a draught of fine English ale with him. Their accommodations in the Tower of London, the fortress Henry had chosen as his home, at least for now, were among the finest to be had. There were servants to attend to their needs, and no shortage of excellent fare to enjoy.

Not a naturally extravagant ruler, Henry was under no illusions regarding who he had to thank for his victory over the Yorkists. He owed his throne to Richard, Stephen, and men of their ilk, and he would not forget it.

"There will be the usual feasting and celebrations to follow the ceremony," Richard muttered in response. "Henry may invite you to dance, and you would do well not to refuse."

"I am a poor dancer, my lord."

"So is he, but you will not find it necessary to mention that, I am sure."

"I shall… Oh, hush, here he is."

Along with the rest of the gathered lords, knights, ladies, and other honoured guests, they fell silent when the great doors opened to admit the king, flanked by his stepfather, Sir William Stanley, and his devoted mother, Margaret Beaufort.

"Do you know those people with the king?" Frances whispered. "Is that his mother? She looks very stern."

"Aye, life has not always been kind to Margaret Beaufort, though I daresay she will consider her suffering a small enough price to pay for her son's throne. She has always been ambitious, and despite Henry having barely any claim at all to the throne, she has worked and schemed tirelessly to promote his cause. She is a most formidable lady, and one I would not wish to cross. As for her husband, Lord Stanley, there are plenty who will say he won Bosworth for Henry by changing sides at the vital moment."

"You do not agree?"

Richard shrugged, never convinced of Lord Stanley's true motives. He rather suspected that the wily nobleman had waited until it was clear which side would win and made sure that was the army he threw his weight behind. There was little doubt, though, that it was Lord Stanley and his men who dragged the defeated King Richard from his horse and hacked him to death on the battlefield, thus sealing the Lancastrian victory.

"The others in the king's group are Lord Stanley's brother, William. And that is Gilbert Talbot, Earl of Shrewsbury."

"Were they also involved in the fighting?"

"Oh, yes. There was barely a nobleman in the land not dragged in on one side or the other. And the man behind Shrewsbury, that is John de Vere, Earl of Oxford."

"What about the older man on the king's right?"

"His uncle, Jasper Tudor. He is the Earl of Pembroke, and as fierce a warrior as you might chance to meet."

"He looks terrifying," Frances murmured.

"He is a force to be reckoned with, certainly. Ah, here is the bride. You will be acquainted with her, I daresay."

Frances nodded. "She is my second cousin. I met her once, several years ago when she and her mother and the young princes stayed at Castle Whitleigh for a few days. Her father was still alive then, of course. Edward the Fourth. After he died, it was thought that she might marry our uncle, King Richard."

"I heard that. It would have been a waste. She is half his age."

"Yes. She is just a couple of months older than I am, so we got on well enough. She is very pretty."

Richard was not about to argue, though he considered it indelicate to agree too profusely. The general view was that Henry was marrying the most beautiful woman of her generation. Even without the massive political advance the match would afford her royal husband, Elizabeth was a prize indeed.

Richard cast a quick glance at his own bride, then again at the future queen. Henry had made a fine bargain, but Richard believed he had done better.

The congregation fell silent as the bride made her slow, graceful way up the aisle to take her place before the altar, at her bridegroom's side. A striking couple, Richard thought. The king was still only twenty-nine years old, and Elizabeth must be about twenty summers if she was so similar in age to Frances. The royal couple made a glittering pair, in the prime of life, ready to found a dynasty.

He wished them luck. God knew, England needed it.

25 January, 1486

The day was cold but clear, and dry. It was just the sort of crisp winter weather that Frances relished, and she had been glad of the opportunity to slip away from the bustle of the court, now relocated to Richmond Palace, to steal a few quiet moments of solitude in the gardens.

Richard was with the king. There was hunting planned, she gathered, and Henry particularly wanted his closest friends about him in these final days before the marriage celebrations ended and the guests all dispersed back to their keeps and castles up and down the land. So, she had the day to herself, provided she might elude the other women of the court.

Frances was naturally gregarious. She enjoyed company and made friends readily enough, but found the court ladies difficult to warm to, especially when encountered en masse. She did not share their passion for fine clothes and nor did she see particular merit in the interminable religious gatherings so beloved of the King's Mother, the Countess of Richmond. The lady was pious beyond imagining, and Frances could not drum up even the remotest enthusiasm for her scholarly ways.

"Do not offend her," had been Richard's warning. "She would make a powerful enemy."

"Why would His Majesty's gracious Lady Mother be interested in my immortal soul?" Frances wondered.

"She considers all souls to be her business. If you do not share her zeal, then you would do well to stay out of her way."

Frances had no quarrel with that as a strategy, and had sought sanctuary in the gardens, though there was little enough to admire at this time of year. She walked along the gravelled paths, inhaled the cool, fresh air, and wondered how long it might be before Richard would consider their courtly duty done and permit them to return to Castle Whitleigh.

The tedium of court life was not the only reason she felt homesick. She had news, important, wondrous, life-changing news. She had not been certain until this last day or so, but there was no remaining doubt. She was to have a child. By the end of the summer, she would be a mother, with her own beautiful baby to cradle in her arms. Her happiness was complete.

She meant to tell Richard this evening and beg him to make his excuses to the king. After her husband, the one other person she longed to share this marvellous news with was her grandmother. Lady Margaret would be so pleased, so excited. Frances could barely wait to see her face when she learned she was to be a great-grandmother.

Lost in her thoughts, Frances turned a corner, then pulled up sharply and dropped into a deep curtsey.

"Your Majesty," she murmured, eyes downcast to focus upon the queen's delicate slippers.

"Ah, Frances. It *is* Frances, is it not?"

Frances rose to her feet. She was surprised to see the queen for once not attended by a gaggle of ladies. "It is, Your Majesty. Frances De Whytte, Duchess of Whitleigh. My husband is Richard, the Duke of Whitleigh."

"Ah, yes, the fearless Sir Richard. My husband speaks highly of him. But you and I have met before, have we not?"

"We have, Your Majesty…"

"Please, call me Elisabeth, since I do believe we are related."

"We are. Your Maj— Elisabeth. We are second cousins, since your father, the late king, was the cousin of my mother."

"Ah, yes. I thought it was something of the sort. And I gather your own wedding took place just recently."

"Eight weeks ago."

"He is a fine man, the duke. I trust you will be happy together, despite your… differences."

"I… I hope so. And you, too, Your Majesty."

"Elisabeth," the queen corrected with a light smile. "We have much in common, you and I. Though I gather you are spared the domineering mother-in law."

Now it was Frances' turn to smile. "My husband just has one brother and no other relatives."

"How fortunate for you. Shall we be seated for a few minutes? These slippers are beautiful, but they pinch my feet dreadfully. There is a secluded bench just around this way, if I remember rightly…"

Bemused, Frances followed the queen, though she had not the slightest notion what they would find to discuss.

They were both very different people now, from the two girls who had giggled over sweetmeats whilst their parents addressed the great issues of the day.

Elisabeth's memory of the layout of the gardens proved to be faultless, and the bench was exactly where she had said. The pair of them settled down, arranged their skirts and their cloaks to ward off the wintry breeze, then gazed off across the barren gardens.

"I always think nature is so bleak at this time of year," the queen observed. "I much prefer the spring, or even the autumn. So much more colour, more vibrancy as everything bursts into life or withdraws into itself for the colder weather to come."

"I love the summer," Frances offered. "The flowers, the birds... Our home, Castle Whitleigh, is surrounded by woodlands, and there are so many squirrels... And bats."

"I am not terribly fond of bats," the queen replied, "though I recall Whitleigh well enough. I would love to visit your home again sometime. Perhaps I will be able to convince the king that we should journey to the south-west."

"That would be wonderful," Frances agreed, and she meant it. Elisabeth of York was just as pleasant a companion as she had remembered. Perhaps they might even be friends...

"You have done as I did, have you not?" the queen continued. "Wed a Lancastrian in order to further my husband's political ambitions."

The change of subject was so sudden that Frances was uncertain how to react. "I... I am not..."

Elisabeth met her gaze. "Let us not beat about the bush. We both know what is at stake here. Our family will only survive if we make this sacrifice."

"I... I suppose that is true. But..."

"They are fine men, though, are they not?" the queen continued, unabashed. "I confess, I was not so keen on the match when it was first suggested two years ago, but as women we have little choice in these matters. It is all about the politics, about power and influence, wealth and property."

Frances's own experience had not been quite so clear-cut, but in general she could not argue with the queen's

177

assessment.

"But that was before I met Henry. It is so nice, do you not agree, so very convenient, when the politics and the personal align?"

"Align, Your Majesty? I am not sure I follow."

The queen shrugged. "It is simple. I love my husband. It does not harm that he is king, despite his insufferable Lady Mother who will insist upon praying for my immortal soul at every opportunity, but I believe I would love him anyway. He makes me laugh. He makes me feel safe, and precious. With him at my side, I can look to the future with enthusiasm. Our children will rule this land, and our union will bring peace to all. Is that not a glittering prize? And does it not shine even more brightly when love it at its heart?"

"Love, Elisabeth?" Frances was struggling to keep up. The queen was sharing something of importance with her, the least she might do was grasp Her Majesty's meaning.

"I love my country. I love my family. I expect you feel the same."

"Of course. Yes."

"And, I love my husband, too."

Well, that at least made sense. "And… I love Richard."

"Indeed. I thought you must, since it is writ plain across your face every time you look at him, and I am quite sure he feels the same. So there we have it, both of us. Politics and personal, in perfect harmony. We are fortunate women, you and I. Our lives and our loves will make a difference. We will help to forge the future."

"I had not thought of it like that before," Frances confessed.

"I can see that you have moved past any initial resentment, as I have. As we must if we are not to be consumed by the past. We cannot change what has gone before, but the future is ours to mould and shape."

"I… I am pregnant," Frances blurted, then covered her mouth with her hand. "Oh, I did not mean to say that. Even Richard does not know yet."

The queen smiled. "Then I am honoured indeed. And you have started already, shaping the future, I mean. My most sincere congratulations and good wishes to you both." She laid her own hand on her stomach. "Since we are trading secrets, I believe I may also be *enceinte*. It is early, still, but perhaps in the late summer…"

"Oh. I am so pleased for you. The king must be delighted."

The queen shook her head. "He does not know yet. We shall keep each other's secrets, you and I, shall we not?"

Frances nodded. "We shall."

The queen got to her feet, and Frances did likewise.

Elisabeth took both Frances' hands in hers. "I am pleased we met and had an opportunity to speak. I had hoped we might, though it is so difficult at court. So many people…"

Frances agreed. "That is why I like to come out here."

"Me, too, but it grows chilly, and I believe it may rain. We should be returning indoors before they come looking for us. Will you walk with me?" The queen offered her arm, and Frances took it. Cousins, and now friends, they strolled back to the palace together.

Richard awaited her in the quarters they shared. Frances was surprised to see him.

"I had thought you would not be back for hours yet." She reached up to kiss him. "Is everything all right?"

He returned her kiss, then hugged her tight. "I love you, you know that."

"Of course. I love you, too."

"I have news," he began.

"As do I. Richard, I—"

"Hush, my love. You need to listen to me." He guided her to a seat by the window. "There has been a message. From Castle Whitleigh."

"A message from home? Why? Has something happened?"

He nodded, his expression one she could not quite name but knew she did not care for at all. For the first time, she noticed that her trunks had been packed. His, too, waited by the door.

"Richard…?

"Sweetheart, I am sorry. So sorry…"

She gazed at him, and a cold knot formed in her stomach as realisation began to dawn. "No," she cried. "Oh dear God, no…"

"I am sorry," he repeated, because after all, there was nothing else. "The message reached me this afternoon whilst I was out with the king. I returned here at once, to find you."

"But how…? Why…?"

"We do not have the details, but there is some shred of comfort to be had. The message came from Sara who was with her when she passed. She sends word that your grandmother died peacefully, in her sleep."

Epilogue
February 1486

"I do not understand how this could have happened. She was not ill. She was strong, and..."

Richard slung an arm across his wife's shoulders. She cut a lonely figure, here beside the newly filled-in grave. The other mourners had all slipped away, their respects paid to the elderly lady who had been born in this house and had died here in her seventy-first year, in the very same bed in which she had come squalling into the world.

Richard was not certain if that denoted a fulfilling existence or not, though there was much to be said for being settled, and for knowing where you belonged. There could be no doubt that Lady Margaret De Whytte had lived and died exactly where, and how, she wanted to be.

No one could really expect more, he concluded.

"Come, it will be dark soon. We should go inside."

"It was so sudden," Frances muttered, as though she had not heard him speak. Perhaps she had not, so wrapped up in her grief as she was. "I do not want to leave her. I should have been here. Maybe if I had been here..."

"Do not say it, Frances. You cannot, must not blame yourself. I shall not permit that, and Lady Margaret would sit up and box your ears if she heard you speaking so. It was her heart, surely. Her time had come. Such matters are the Lord's to determine, not yours, not mine."

"I know that, but... I shall miss her so."

"We will all miss her. She was a fine lady, one of the gentlest I ever met. And the wisest."

Frances slanted a tear-filled glance up at him. "You know, I would not have wed you but for her advice. She rarely told me what to do, but on that occasion..."

"I am glad you heeded her words."

"Me, too." She slipped her hand into his. "Thank you for waiting. I just wanted a few moments alone."

"Are you ready to come inside now?"

Frances nodded, and together they turned to walk back up the hillside towards the castle drawbridge.

"Your brother is gone, and now your grandmother, but you are not alone in the world."

"I know that."

"Apart from me, there is Stephen, too, though he will spend much of his time at Keeterly from now on."

"I have other family, too. The queen, for one. She remembered me, and we spoke. She wants to visit…"

"We would be honoured."

"And, there is more…" She paused and turned to face him. "I was going to tell you, before we left Richmond Palace, but everything became such a blur."

"Tell me what, sweetheart?"

"My family… Our family…" She laid her hand on her stomach.

Richard's dark eyes widened. "You mean…? Are you…?"

Frances nodded. "In July, I think. I must speak to Betsy. She will be able to work it out."

Richard beamed at her and lifted her from her feet. He swung her around, set her down, and planted a kiss on her lips. "If it is a girl, we shall call her Margaret. There should always be a Margaret at Castle Whitleigh."

August 1486

He paced the hall, cringing with every shriek echoing from the bedchamber above. Who would have imagined that his sweet, quiet Frances could possibly make so much din? And it was all his fault. Even as Richard rejoiced — for after all, was this not the most joyous of occasions? — he loathed himself for inflicting such misery upon the woman he adored.

Never again, he promised himself. *Never again.*

The caterwauling ceased. All was silent. Richard stopped pacing and turned to where his brother lounged at the table. Despite his casual demeanour, Stephen was almost as anxious as Richard was.

"I should go up," Richard avowed, for what must

have been the hundredth time. "She needs me…"

"Betsy will only throw you out. Again. Leave it to the women. They understand such matters."

His brother's counsel was sound, but Richard found the silence to be even more deafening than his wife's screams. He could bear it no longer. "I shall go to her…"

He was on the fourth step when Betsy appeared at the top of the stairs, a bundle in her arms.

Richard halted. "Is that…?"

"Your son, my lord. You have a son. A fine boy…"

As if to demonstrate the accuracy of her words, the infant chose that moment to let out a shrill cry.

Richard took the rest of the stairs two at a time. He peered down at the pink face, contorted in apparent anguish. "May I?"

Betsy handed the bundle to him, and Richard inserted the tip of his little finger into the tiny mouth. The cries ceased, and the baby tried to suckle.

"He is hungry. He needs his mama. I shall take him back now. Her ladyship was so keen that we bring him to show you at once…"

Richard would have handed the baby back, but both he and Betsy went stock-still at another ear-splitting scream from within the duke's chamber.

"What? But I thought it was all over…" Richard was bewildered, and, from her startled expression, Betsy equally so.

"It is. It was." The woman spun around and scurried back along the corridor.

Richard followed, still clutching his newborn son to his chest. The sight that greeted him was one he had hoped never to witness.

Frances writhed on the bed, her legs splayed and the sheet beneath her stained with blood.

"Dear God!" Richard handed his son to a maidservant hovering close by. "Take care of him." He rushed to the bedside and grasped his wife's flailing hand. "Frances, my darling. I am here…"

"Richard…?" she croaked. "What is happening? Our

son…?"

"He is fine. A beautiful boy. He needs his mama, though…"

"I know. I want… I… Aaaaagh!" Her face contorted in agony, and she planted her feet firmly on the mattress.

"Betsy, what is going on? What is wrong?" he demanded as Frances' grip on his hand increased to resemble a vice.

"It would seem she is still in labour, my lord." Betsy lifted the stained sheet and peered beneath. "Ah, I see it…"

"See it? See what, for fuck's sake?" Frances' deathly grip eased somewhat, and she flopped back against the pillow.

"The second one," came the calm reply. "We have twins, my lord."

"Twins?" Beyond astonished, Richard rallied sufficiently to sweep the lank hair from his wife's face.

She opened her eyes and blinked up at him.

"It hurts…"

"I know. I know, sweetheart, but it will soon be over. There is a second child still to come."

"Another….?"

"Aye. A twin."

"I… Oh… Aaaagh!" She was gripped by the next contraction, and once again planted her feet and pushed. This time, though, Richard was there to encourage. Betsy, too.

"You are doing well, my lady. 'Tis almost here. I have the head…"

Dear Lord, if you have any mercy at all, help us. And do not let me pass out now.

Richard had never been so terrified. He would rather face a thousand deadly foes on the battlefield than this uniquely human drama. Yet here he was, in it up to his armpits, almost literally. He managed not to wince too much when Frances threatened to crush every bone in his hand, managing instead to dab her forehead with a damp cloth someone thrust at him.

"Almost there. My darling…."

"One more push," Betsy announced. "With the next

contraction you need to—"

"I damned well know what to do," Frances snapped, "I just… aaagh!"

The world tipped into slow motion. He was convinced his hand must be crumbling beneath the pressure. Frances let out an unearthly howl, her features twisted into a grimace, her chin tucked into her chest while she heaved for all she was worth.

"I have it. 'Tis here…" Betsy emerged from beneath the blanket, a look of triumph on her ruddy face and a slippery scrap of humanity cradled in both her hands. "This one is a bit smaller, but…"

The newborn let out a faint squeal.

"Is it all right?" Frances gasped. "What is it?"

He peered for a moment at the baby, still covered in blood, and he did not care to think what else. "It's a little girl," Richard replied as the squeaks escalated to a raucous shriek. "And she sounds all right to me."

"A girl," Frances echoed.

"Aye. Castle Whitleigh has another Margaret. And we shall name the lad Henry, for the king, and Edmund for his uncle."

"Margaret, and Henry Edmund. Yes, those are fine names." Despite her weakness, Frances reached for her daughter. "I should feed her, but the boy has been waiting longer…"

"He will have to become accustomed to seeing his baby sister spoiled rotten," Richard replied, "but I think we should find a wet nurse even so."

"There is a woman in the village," Betsy said. "I thought we might have need of her, so I took the liberty of speaking with her already. Sara, run and find Mistress Milton. Just had her sixth, she has, and producing more milk than a prize heifer."

Richard swallowed hard. Surely, he had been exposed to quite enough female biology for one day. "Maybe I should leave you all to…"

Frances grabbed at his sleeve. "No," she whispered. "Please, stay. I am not so frightened when you are here."

"I should have come upstairs earlier."

"I wish you had."

It was not a mistake he would make again. Richard sighed and walked around to the other side of the bed, then eased himself up onto the mattress beside his wife. He took the whimpering baby boy from the maidservant who had been entrusted with his care during the crisis. The doting new father smiled down at the grumpy infant in his arms. "Ah, young Henry, I fear you and I must both wait our turn from now on. Little Lady Margaret has arrived."

Thank you for reading *Right of Conquest.* If you enjoyed the story, I would really appreciate it if you would leave a review. Reviews are invaluable to indie authors in helping us to market our books and they provide useful feedback to help us work even harder to bring you more of the stories you love.

About the Author

USA Today best-selling author Ashe Barker has been an avid reader of fiction for many years, erotic and other genres. She still loves reading, the hotter the better. But now she has a good excuse for her guilty pleasure – research.

Ashe lives in the North of England, on the edge of the Brontë moors and enjoys the occasional flirtation with pole dancing and drinking Earl Grey tea. When not writing – which is not very often these days - her time is divided between caring for a menagerie of dogs, tortoises, gerbils And a very grumpy cockatiel.

At the last count Ashe had around sixty titles on general release with publishers on both sides of the Atlantic, and several more in the pipeline. She writes M/f, M/M, and occasionally rings the changes with a little M/M/f. Ashe's books invariably feature BDSM. She writes explicit stories, always hot, but offering far more than just sizzling sex. Ashe likes to read about complex characters, and to lose herself in compelling plots, so that's what she writes too.

Ashe has a pile of story ideas still to work through and keeps thinking of new ones at the most unlikely moments, so you can expect to see a lot more from her.

Also by Ashe Barker

The Black Combe Doms
Dark Melodies
Sure Mastery
Hard Limits
Laid Bare

Black Combe Doms Box Set

The Skye Duet
Book 1 Highland Odyssey
Book 2 Above and Beyond

Contemporary
A Dom is for Life
Innocent
Broken
Tell Me
Her Two Doms (also in audiobook)
Capri Heat
Making The Rules
Faith
Spirit
Hardened
First Impressions
The Three Rs
Chameleon
La Brat

Historical
Deeds Not Words
The Laird and the Sassenach

Sassenach Bride
Seducing His Sassenach
Wolfeheart (De Wolfe Pack Connected World)
Her Celtic Masters
Conquered by the Viking
Her Rogue Viking
Her Dark Viking
Her Celtic Captor
The Widow is Mine (The Conquered Brides collection)
A Scandalous Arrangement
The Highwayman's Lady
Her Noble Lords

Sci-fi
Her Alien Commander
Theirs: Found and Claimed

Paranormal and Time Travel
Resurrection
Shared by the Highlanders
Held In Custody
Under Viking Dominion

LGBT
Gideon
Bodywork
Hard Riders

Short Stories and Novellas
Viking Surrender (The Prologue) (also in audiobook)
Brandr (Viking Surrender, Book 1) (also in audiobook)
A Tale of Two Pirates
Brigands, Thieves and Lawless Ladies
Rough Diamonds
Re-Awakening

Carrot and Coriander
In the Eyes of the Law
The Prize
A Very Private Performance
Yes or No?
Rose's Are Red

Printed in Great Britain
by Amazon

54561819R00108